"It's Gibson Duke, Ma'am."

Sarah recognized the rider then, and came from behind the bush, holding the carbine high.

"Don't be unfriendly, ma'am," he said.

"Look, Mr. Duke," Sarah replied, "I don't need help and I don't need a man. If I see you again, I'll shoot you down like a rattlesnake. There was only one man—and he's dead. I ain't after another."

She snapped her pony around and sent it splashing through the stream. She did not look back.

Duke rolled a cigarette and raised one leg over the pommel of his saddle. He smoked slowly, and when he was finished, he wheeled the black into the stream and began slowly trotting after Sarah Phelps.

Fawcett Gold Medal Books
by Richard Jessup:

COMANCHE VENGEANCE
TEXAS OUTLAW

Comanche Vengeance

by Richard Jessup

A FAWCETT GOLD MEDAL BOOK
Fawcett Books, Greenwich, Conn.

COMANCHE VENGEANCE

© 1957 CBS Publications, The Consumer Publishing Division of CBS, Inc. All Rights Reserved

All characters in this book are fictional and any resemblance to persons living or dead is purely coincidental.

Printed in the United States of America

15 14 13 12 11 10 9 8 7 6

THE MORNING was bright and hard when Adam Phelps opened the door to his sturdy cabin near the outer rim of the Texas Brazos. His stomach filled with cornbread and sowbelly, coffee that was black and hot and sweet. He knocked out his pipe and let his eye travel along the line of rail fencing that separated the yard from the outer range. There were three outhouses. A chicken coop and pen, shed for the horses and a milking shed for Elvira and Nancy, their two milking Jerseys.

His eyes were soft and friendly. The great eastern sun had risen again and there it was. Paint it up a little bit, he thought, and it would be a picture from a book. As far as his eye could see there were oceans of grass. Beyond a slight rise to the west Adam Phelps knew there were forty-five head of the finest cattle, grazing contentedly.

"Git going, Adam," a warm voice said from inside the house. "It's be just like you to stand there all day dreaming about how pretty it is." Mrs. Phelps came to stand in back of her husband and look out on the scene. "And I can't say that I'd blame you at all." She sighed. "Git now!" she said, giving her husband a mock shove into the yard.

Adam turned and grinned at his wife. "Woman, stop

manhandling me. Remember who I am. Captain Adam Phelps, Georgia Fourteenth Cavalry." He came to attention and saluted.

"Git on with you," Sarah Phelps said. "And mind, don't you go riding out over that northern trace. You know well as I do that old One Nest took them steers—and you ain't going to find nothing but trouble if you go looking for 'em."

The friendly light in Adam's eyes hardened. His teeth clamped together. "You tend to the children, ma'am, and I'll handle the running of our spread."

"Promise me," Sarah said. She matched her husband's hardness.

Adam Phelps turned on his heel and strode to the shed. Sarah watched him as he saddled up the roan, and with a wave and grin trotted to the front gate.

She stood a long time watching the rider move straight across the grass until he was lost in the wild green of the Brazos headwaters. She sighed and turned back to her house and the problems of the day.

A six-year-old girl, tall, like her mother, with yellow hair and bright blue eyes, was playing with a rag doll. "Time to go see if the chickens have done anything, Little Sue," Sarah said to her daughter. And then turning to a three and a half year old boy, she patted him on the shoulder. "Hurry now, Buster, git your breakfast down. I want you to help me make the butter today."

Sarah turned to the hand pump and primed it carefully with half a bucket of water, then with a vigorous action began pumping the water up. The rusty clanking of the handle on the socket filled the two-room house with sound. The water came up and Sarah dragged the butter churn over and began to fill it up.

"Git going now, Little Sue," she said. She took a bar of lye soap and dropped it into the churn, and with a brush made of boar hair began scrubbing out the butter maker. "Go on, now, Sue, girl," she said. "Don't want the hens to think they can sit on them eggs."

Reluctantly the girl moved toward the door, taking her doll with her. "Just leave that doll right here," Sarah Phelps said, elbow-deep in the strong water. "You can't collect eggs with a doll in one hand and a basket in the other."

"I'll go, Mama," Buster said. "Can I help Little Sue?"

"All right, go ahead," Sarah said.

The two children left the house together and Sarah Phelps bent to the task of cleaning out the butter churn.

Sarah thought about the day as she scrubbed the inside of the wooden churn; it was like many others since they had packed up and left Savannah, traveling west. "We'll just keep going, Sarah, until we find the right place," Adam had told her. "The right place will speak to us. High or low, green or brown, dry or wet, Sarah Phelps, the right place will rise right up and tell us. 'This is your resting place.' That's where we'll light."

Sarah stopped scrubbing momentarily and looked out the window. The grass was high, and it looked as if there might be a good soft winter instead of the blistering cold of the last three. And there were now forty-five head of cattle instead of the six they had brought with them. Another day, she thought, returning to her scrubbing, of waiting for Adam to come home, of waiting for the night and waiting for the morning and waiting for the winter and waiting for the spring and the summer. But deep in her soul, the scars of the Georgia ruin of their home by Sherman's raiders was slowly being eased away by this new life.

She was a tall woman, nearing thirty, and her hands were nearly as tough as her husband's. But she still kept herself up. She did that for herself mostly, but she also knew that she did it for Adam. She loved to watch his eyes roam over her when the children were in bed and the light was burning low. She knew that there was little enough in his life and the least she could do was keep herself looking up for him. But she would never in this world let him know that!

The scrubbing was over. She began dipping the water out of the churn and pouring it out of the sluice Adam had built to drain off water from the pump basin. Another day, she thought, and the children are growing up fine.

She threw the last of the water out of the churn and began pumping in fresh water to rinse it out. The children had been gone a long time. She stopped and walked to the door. "Sue! Little Sue!"

Silence, except for the slight rustle of the winds over the grass and around the yard. She wiped her hands on her apron and pushed back a wisp of hair from her forehead. She stepped into the yard and walked toward the chicken coop. "Little Sue! Answer me!"

Something gripped her heart. It was as if a voice had suddenly encased the organ and would not let it continue to beat. She began to hasten her steps. "Buster— Little Sue! Answer me. I'll whip you children if there's any foolishness going on. Answer me!"

She was across the yard now. She was near the edge of the coop when she screamed. On the ground, at the edge of the little greasewood thatch hut, she saw the relaxed hand of her son, white and still.

She made the corner of the coop in one leap and stopped in horror. Her children were sprawled on the ground, Buster's red skull already half covered with flies. Little Sue was bent double, backwards. Comanche arrows were buried in both their bodies.

Sarah Phelps felt herself falling and reached out to hang on to the coop, but she never made it. She fainted dead away, falling a few feet from the body of her scalped three-year-old son.

Sarah opened her eyes. She stared into the blue sky and heard the distant pounding of hoofbeats. There had been such a bad dream. "Adam—" she said softly, "I had a terrible dream."

She felt the hard ground under her and then heard the clucking of the chickens. She screamed, her eyes wide open, she let out a blood-curdling cry that filled her ears and obliterated every sound and the thing that she knew to be real.

She fought with herself to turn her head. She bit her tongue, lying there, staring at the sky, watching a hawk circle, and felt the front teeth sink into her tongue, but the pain was not enough to take away the thought, the fact that she knew was true and she finally turned her head.

Sarah Phelps fainted again.

When Sarah awakened the second time, she moved at once. She got up and took the bodies of her children in her arms and carried them into the house.

Everything was the same. The churn was there, half filled with rinse water, the dishes left from the sourbelly breakfast. She began to cry, softly, the tears streaming down her face, as she took each body and tenderly began to take out the arrows.

She stopped often, closed her eyes and gritted her teeth so hard the pain shot up into her temples, but she carried on. She removed the children's clothes and washed them carefully, tenderly. Not once did she speak. She did not look around her. After a long while, she stopped crying.

She took Little Sue's best dress out of the chest and slipped it over the child's body. Then she put Buster's little sailor suit on him that had been made from an old suit of clothes worn out by Adam. When she finished, she looked around her and saw that it was growing dark.

The chickens were making noises and there was a low moaning from the cowshed where the Jersey cows demanded attention. There were the usual sighing breezes from the winds over the grass, and the cries of the hawks.

Sarah heard none of these things. She moved to the table, sat down on the hard bench holding a hand of each child, and waited for Adam.

CHAPTER TWO

THE ROAN did not come back for two days. Sarah had not moved. The horse stood at the gate of the dooryard and waited, pawing the earth and crying, but Sarah did not move. She sat, still holding the hands of her children, staring into nothingness and the vacuum of hell. There was hardly any sign of her breathing.

The chickens had long ago flown over the edges of the coop fence and scattered around the outer fields of grass. The Jerseys had broken loose and bawled around the yard and they also broke out of the fence and buried their faces in the grass.

Sarah Phelps moved at last. She got up with the stiffness of two days' sitting and moved, unaware of her own body, out to the gate where the roan waited. It was night and the stars were high, but they seemed like Christmas tree ornaments and close enough to touch. She opened the gate and looked at the saddle. Blood had dried on the cantle and flap. She patted the roan on the nose and led it into the enclosure, removed the saddle and sat in the door with the heavy Western saddle across her lap, smoothing and smoothing out the blood of her husband.

She looked up at the roan. "Why didn't they kill me, too," she said softly. The animal jerked up at the strange sound of a voice after so many days of silence, and then returned to the grass.

Sarah dug the two little graves for Little Sue and Buster with care. She dug deep and had to use a ramp to get in and out of the graves. When she could no longer throw dirt out of the hole, she went into the house and took the bodies of her children and wrapped them in the best blankets she had, returned to the graves, and buried them.

When it was over, she dropped the shovel and turned back to the house. She did not make the bed. She fell across the doorstep and slept for the rest of that night and all the next day and deep into the next night.

When she awoke, she got up and pumped water into a pot and made herself a cup of strong tea. She ate a little bread and drank a little whisky from the crock taken from the earthen cellar.

The whisky made her a little ill and dizzy, but she expected that. She drank more coffee and took another long drink of the whisky. Then, with her sewing scissors, she cut off her long black hair until it was just off the neck. She let the hair lay where it fell on the floor, and stripped off her clothes.

Naked, she took another drink of whisky from the crock and then turned to the chest, where she pulled out a pair of trousers that had been too small for her husband and that she had been saving for Buster. She slipped them on and put on a thick shirt. A thick winter jumper Adam had used for the winter was thrown to the table. She stuffed the legs of the pants into the tops of her flat-heeled boots and took another drink from the crock.

It was nearly dawn when Sarah had finished packing her blanket roll. And the last of the whisky in the crock was gone. She felt around the inner lining of the chest and pulled out a small leather sack of gold coins. She shoved them into her pocket without opening it. She knew there were eighteen double eagles.

With the sun breaking over the eastern hump of the Brazos, Sarah pulled out the heavy Colt and belt that had been her father's, and strapped it on. The weight was uncomfortable, but she did not appear to notice it. From over the fireplace she took a carbine and shoved a double box of shells into the blanket roll.

The last thing she took before moving out of the house was the small three-sided picture of her husband, her mother and father. They had not had a chance to have pictures taken of their children.

She called the roan, saddled it and slipped the carbine into the leather on the flap. She swung into the saddle and looked around at the buildings, her eyes dead and flat. She got off the pony, went back into the house, studied it a moment and went to the fireplace. She took the flint and struck a light to shavings and in a moment, the fire was glowing. She took a burning stick and went around the room setting fire to anything that would catch and then walked outside to the coop, cowshed and horse stalls. She called to the roan, slipped into the saddle. She rode into the grass, stopped and watched the buildings burn. They burned for nearly two hours, high, billowing flames that leaped into the bright morning sun, and then slowly grew smaller and smaller until the buildings were gone and there was nothing left but charred remains.

She whipped the roan around and loped across the grass toward the traces where she knew she would find the body of her husband.

"I'm sorry, Adam," she said softly, standing bareheaded over the freshly dug grave. "I would blow my brains out now and lie down with you—if—" She did not continue.

She dropped to one knee and closed her eyes. She prayed silently. She remounted the roan and stood for a moment, looking down at the grave. "Goodby, Adam Phelps. I loved you."

She whipped the pony around, lashed it hard on the rump and rode high and fast into the west, along the traces where she knew the Comanche had taken the herd of cattle.

Sarah rode until nightfall, stopped beside a stream in the upper watershed of the Brazos. She did not make a fire. She took the saddle off the roan and staked him out near the water and lay down on her blanket and closed her eyes. She did not think about Adam Phelps or her son and daughter. That had been shoved out of her mind. She began to think about everything she had ever heard about the Comanche and their habits and ways.

She went to sleep finally with the image of Chief One Nest in her mind. A deep-eyed, heavy-nosed Indian with stringy black hair that fell loosely in a fan on his shoulders. A tall Indian with huge hands and a green cast to his eyes.

Sarah had seen him once. When he came to ask for food, slyly using the pretext of begging to look them over. Adam had been generous and given him a steer for his lodge, and the Indian had ridden away leading the steer without thanking them.

She remembered stories about Comanche and their ways, different from the other plains Indians in one outstanding feature. They moved constantly—that she had heard in her semiannual visits with Adam to the post down the Brazos. They loved women, she remembered. The braves were particularly demanding on their women. They were merciless and they were never to be trusted. Different from the Apache, who had a fierce pride and would face his foe over a blade. And they were different from the Cheyenne to the north, who were resilient, warlike, and with even more pride than the Apache, and the finest horsemen in the world. But the Comanche, unlike the Apache and the Cheyenne, could not be trusted when he gave his word.

On and on, she thought back to the difference in the Comanche and the others, remembering small details of gossip and bulling she had heard while shopping in the post grocery store, and the stories that Adam told her.

Piece by piece she put together a pattern of their behavior and their likes and dislikes. She saw the one image of the chief of this tribe; One Nest, who had slain her husband, scalped a three-year-old boy and violated a six-year-old girl.

But she did not sleep, deeply, or for very long. Throughout the night she woke up and jerked into a sitting position to stare around her in the darkness before she remembered where she was, who she was and what she was doing there.

Then, when she remembered, she would push the images of what had happened out of her mind and return to thoughts of a long-haired Indian, tall, with a green shading to his eyes.

CHAPTER THREE

SARAH searched the traces in the watershed for three days. She backtracked, crisscrossing her own trail, often studying hoofprints only to discover that they were those of her own roan. She left the headwater's region and turned back toward the post along the Brazos banks. It was near the end of a week after her leaving that she found a cattle trail. Her heart leaped with sudden fury. She jerked the roan around and began following the trail that was bending toward the post. She could not believe that the Indian would dare take the stolen cattle anywhere near the settlement, but the tracks were plain and clear. She spurred her roan, and on the flat, level land, raced after the tracks of more than fifty cattle. And there were the unmistakable ruts of a dragging travois. Indians, all right.

Late that night, Sarah rode into the post, still following the trail of cattle and travois ruts. Near the edge of town she found a pen full of the bawling steers. She got off the roan, slipped through the fence and started to examine the brand of the nearest animal.

"Just get right out of there, mister!" a voice commanded behind Sarah.

Sarah straightened up, turned slowly and faced a burly man with a beard and overhanging stomach above the cinch of his gunbelt. "Where'd you git these cattle?" she demanded.

"I said git out of there." The man pulled a Colt and cocked it. "Now you coming, or do I drag you out?"

Sarah moved slowly toward the fence and stepped outside. The man stepped in close, gun still high, and examined Sarah closely in the darkening light. "You got business with them cattle, you talk to me first."

"They belong to you?" Sarah asked.

The man stared. "You look like a man, but you sound like a woman. Which is it?"

Several hands moved in around the fence and listened, watching Sarah and the man who still held his gun high.

"Where did you get those cattle?" Sarah demanded.

14

"My. My, I believe we are a woman!" The man pulled at the wide-brimmed hat and Sarah's hair, though cropped short, easily identified her as a woman.

"It's Sarah Phelps," someone said.

"What's she done to herself!"

The man laughed and put his gun away. "I'm sorry, lady, if I scared you, but any time I see a pistol-toting man looking over my cows, I just naturally get skittish."

No sooner had the man's gun slipped into the holster than Sarah drew the heavy Colt fast and sure and rammed it into the man's gut. Her jaw was hard. "Mister," she said, "them cows belonged to me and my husband last week. They grazed just west of here on the headlands grass. Now you tell me where you got 'em or I'll blow your guts out right here."

The man paled. The voices around Sarah murmured. The man looked wildly around him. "Stop her, somebody, she's gone loco."

"Where did you get them cows!"

"I bought 'em," the man said. "I paid over twenty dollars a head for 'em last Tuesday."

"Who from?"

"An Indian."

"What Indian?" Sarah demanded.

"Lady, I don't know what Indian," the man said, his eyes on the Colt. "I was riding up from Dade when I seen high dust below the river line. I crossed over, thinking it might be a freighter coming into the post and I could rest from the saddle. It turns out that it was a village of Indians, and they had these cattle. I tried to avoid them, but they sent out a rider and asked me if I was interested in buying them. I was suspicious, but I bought 'em anyway."

"Can you prove that?"

"Well—hell, Lady, why do I have to prove anything to you?"

"Because I got a Colt shoved in your gut, that's why," Sarah said. "Where's your proof?"

"I didn't get no receipt, or nothing—lady. Goddam, don't you know how it is with Indians?"

"These cattle were stolen from me," Sarah said, her voice hard. "And my daughter and son and husband were all killed."

The crowd around them murmured at this news. Sarah ignored them. She still had the gun pressed tightly into the man's belly. "I'm going to count ten, mister, and you better come up with some proof." Sarah began to count.

The man looked around at the others. "You folks don't know me, but—I—you can't let her shoot a man down in cold blood—"

"—five—six—" Sarah counted slowly.

"I ain't got no proof!"

A figure moved in from the darkness and the outer edges of the crowd. "Drop that gun, miss," a harsh voice said. There was the unmistakable click of a Colt being cocked.

Sarah jerked the man before her with her free hand and spun around to the back of him. She fired once. A man screamed. The Colt fell to the ground. The cattle owner, in the movement's respite, tried to pull his own gun. Sarah backhanded him across the face with the barrel of her own Colt and sent the man down against the cattle pen.

"Get back!" Sarah said, backing up against the pen and raising the Colt against the crowd. "This is for everybody. And listen good. My daughter was violated, and she wasn't but six years old. My son was scalped and he wasn't but three and a half. My husband was scalped and had his stomach ripped open and sand poured into his innards. I had to bury them all with my own hands. Do any of you want to protect this man—or try and stop me?"

The crowd did not move. They stared in open-mouthed stupefaction at the short hair and grime streaked face of Sarah Phelps, and they were silent. The Colt of the intruding man still lay on the ground. The man held his wrist where Sarah's bullet had shattered the bone.

She kicked the cattle owner in the side. "Git up." she commanded. "I'm still counting."

The man began to cry. "Lady—what do I have to do to prove it? I got letters from folks back in Dade that sent me up here to see about a business proposition. I got a spread of my own down south of Brazos—"

"What did this Indian that you bought the cattle look like?" Sarah said, cutting him off. "That's a way of proving it. There ain't but one Indian that coulda done it.'

"He was just an Indian!"

"Was he short?"

The man hesitated and bit his lip. "No, ma'am, he was tall."

"Did he wear a pigtail?" Sarah prompted.

The man glanced around at the crowd.

Sarah rammed the gun in his neck. "Did he wear a pigtail!"

"No, ma'am. His hair was in a fan around his shoulders."

"What else?"

"He had large hands—"

Sarah nodded. "All right, mister. I guess you did buy them." She turned and spoke to the roan. The animal came toward her and she swung into the saddle. "I could go to court and take them critters back from you," she said. "But courts don't mean much to me now."

She slapped hard on the roan's haunch and broke through the crowd and headed out of the post. She would have to backtrack and find out where the trail separated, where One Nest had gone on with his village and where the cattle had been brought into the post.

She left the settlement moving fast and hard into the night.

Back at the stream where she had first picked up the trail, Sarah began scouting the edges. She rode far to the south and north of the banks, scanning the shore line for any sign of tracks or travois ruts. She worked the banks all day, slipping in and out of the water when any overhang or brush made it impossible for her to continue at the shore line.

By nightfall she had not found a single track, except where the cattle had come up on the opposite bank.

They came up the river, she concluded. They worked their way up the river after driving them from the trace and off the graze. They coulda made their bargaining right back there in the water, she thought, sitting with one leg up on the pommel of her saddle. And the village coulda moved on up the river itself.

It was full dark before she decided to head up the

Brazos, but in her heart she knew the trail would be lost. The headwaters had hundreds of little streams in the watershed area, any number of them large enough to protect the trails of a whole village.

She rode north in the water, talking low to the roan, not feeling the tired ache that ran up her spine or the heavy strain of spending too much time in the saddle.

When she woke up from a catnap she had fallen into while riding, she knew it was useless to continue that night. She pulled the roan off the edge of the stream and into a brush-covered area.

She made herself some coffee and ate leather-tough deer jerky taken from the earthen cellar of their cabin, and stretched out to sleep on the hard ground. It did not even occur to Sarah Phelps to unroll the blanket. . . .

For five days Sarah searched the streams of the headwaters of the Brazos without finding the trail. She stopped looking in the middle of one hot sunny afternoon and broke away from the area completely. If the Comanche chief had sold the cattle for twenty dollars a head, there was every possibility that he might eventually stop at some trading post. And since the village had to have been along the way, there was a good chance they would follow the buffalo track taken by the few remaining herds of the once great Texas herd.

She would start, she decided, by following the buffalo trail herself. She headed the roan north, slanting a little toward the North Wichita and the little town of Lister.

CHAPTER FOUR

GIBSON DUKE rode his black wearily. He had been moving too long for one stretch. All the way down from the Montana highlands and through the jagged country of Wyoming into Nebraska and the North Platte, leaving it and heading straight south for the Kansas flats and the Texas Panhandle. He was a thickset man, with black hair and a hard face. He wore his Colt tied low. A carbine in the leather at his knee was old and well oiled and kept that way by a leather cover across the butt stock.

He rode into Lister, Texas, and hoped there would be a decent hotel and restaurant. As it turned out, there was neither. A rooming house, the sheriff had told him, offered the best there was in the town. He had dropped the black off at the livery and walked down to the end of the store fronts carrying his saddlebags and carbine.

"You going to be in town long, Mr. Duke?" asked the flat-nosed girl who took his seven dollars advance for one week.

"Never can tell," he said. "If I like the smell of your place, I might do that."

"You a cattleman or a digger, Mr. Duke?" the young girl asked, a pretty smile on her lips.

"My, you're about the nosiest thing to be so pretty I ever saw." Gibson Duke smiled, patted her on the head and climbed wearily to the upper floor and stripped for a hot bath.

He was nearly asleep in the hot tub when there was a knock on the door. "Supper's ready, Mr. Duke."

Duke put on his one clean shirt and pulled on the dirty pants reluctantly. He strapped on the Colt, tied it down carefully, tested it and spun it lightly on his finger. He dropped it into his leather and turned to the door. He was at the top step when he smelled the tantalizing odor of pork chops and biscuits and closed his eyes. He walked down the steps slowly, enjoying the aroma of the food, and tripped suddenly and fell headlong. He grabbed wildly for the bannister, missed it and would have fallen on his face at the bottom of the stairs if a strong pair of hands had not grabbed him.

"Thanks, mister," he said, straightening up. "Smell of good food just about took me out."

Sarah nodded and swept past him, climbing the stairs quickly. Gibson Duke examined the retreating figure carefully, noting the slightness of the shoulders, but took special note of the low-slung, tied-down Colt. He could not help but reflect on the prettiness of the face.

"She's a woman, not a man," said the little girl. "Fooled you, didn't she?"

"A—woman!" Duke turned to look up the deserted stairway. "Well, I'll be damned."

The young girl giggled at the profanity and hurried into the kitchen.

Sarah sat at the table, head down, opposite Gibson Duke. They were the only diners and Mrs. Cotten and Josey ate with them.

"Josey tells me you might be staying in Lister, Mr. Duke," Mrs. Cotten, a huge, warm, happy-faced woman, said.

"I may," Duke said, "and I mayn't." He glanced at Sarah. "You don't come from around here, I reckon, ma'am," he said.

Sarah shook her head.

"This just a stopover?"

Sarah looked up and stared him in the eye. She did not reply.

"Tyrone Mishcorte is our sheriff," Mrs. Cotten said to both of them. "He likes to meet strangers that come into Lister."

"I reckon I haven't got anything to hide, ma'am." he said softly. He offered Sarah the pork chops.

"No," Sarah said. She turned her head to Mrs. Cotten. "Have there been any Comanches through here lately?"

"Comanche Indians?" Mrs. Cotten asked, surprised.

Sarah nodded. "Indians. Have there been any in town lately with a lot of money?"

"Well, I don't know. But Mr. Mishcorte would surely know. You might ask him."

"Looking for Indians, ma'am?" Duke asked.

"Yes. Have you seen any Comanches on your ride down from the flats?"

"Well—a few here and there," Duke said cautiously. "Any particular ones you interested in?"

Sarah nodded. "I'll ask the sheriff. Where can I find him?"

"Down the street, last building on your right," Mrs. Cotten said. "He'll be there now. He's eating dinner. He takes some of his meals with me, but dinner is sent over to his office."

Sarah nodded and got up. When she had left the house, Duke stood up stretched and patted his belly. "Ma'am, that was as good a meal as I've eaten in many days."

He took his hat and hurried out of the house and into the street. Down the line, he could see the small lithe figure of Sarah walking quickly.

"No ma'am, there ain't been an Indian, Comanche or other kind, in Lister for a few months—especially any with money. They usually come through here begging for one thing or another, outcasts from their village and general no-accounts." The sheriff eyed the strange figure of Sarah Phelps. "Why you askin', ma'am?"

Sarah hesitated. "I got a reason, Sheriff."

"Yessum, I reckon you have."

The door opened and Gibson Duke entered. "How do, Sheriff." He nodded to Sarah. "I just thought of something that this lady might be interested in."

"What's that?" Sarah asked.

"Well, you askin' about Comanche. I nearly forgot about that little bunch that I rode past the other day." He watched Sarah closely.

"How many were there?"

"About fifty or more, I reckon," Duke said. "They were just north of here, moving toward Red River."

Sarah's eyes glowed hotly. "North toward Red River, you say?"

"Yessum. They were Comanche, too."

Sarah turned back to the sheriff. "Thank you, sir," she said. Facing Duke, she smiled. "Thank you, mister." She put her hand out for the door. Duke stepped in front of her.

"Ma'am, I wouldn't go messing around no Comanche," he said hurriedly. "They can't be trusted as far as you can throw a buffalo bull. More especially since you're a woman, ma'am."

Sarah dropped her hand. "Thank you for your consideration, but if you'll let me pass, I'll be on my way." Her voice was hard, cold and level.

Duke withdrew his hand and nodded. "There's one thing you oughtta know about this particular bunch of Comanche," he said lightly. "They belong to old Kaygeesee's bunch. They don't like visitors."

"When I visit," Sarah said, "they won't know anything about it until I'm gone."

"Yessum," Duke said. "Good luck to you, ma'am."

Sarah passed through the door and disappeared into the darkness of the street. Duke pursed his lips. "Now what you reckon she wants to go huntin' up Comanche for?"

"You get me," Mishcorte said, throwing up his hands. "That Colt looked as big as a cannon, and she don't look strong enough to pull it out."

"Wonder where she's from?" Duke said, thoughtfully, digging into a tooth with a toothpick. "She's wearing a wedding ring. You don't reckon she's after some Injuns that's kilt her husband or something, now do you?"

"I'd stop her, if there was someway to do it." Mishcorte said. "Cause it's suicide for her to ride into a Comanche camp."

Duke nodded. There was something appealing about that woman. He grinned. "Now, you know, Sheriff, every town like this one has a town ordinance about carrying guns."

"Sure—but I ain't going to enforce it. I'm just here to keep drunks from shooting up the town—and I ain't thinking about nothing else."

"Why, hell, man, you can save that woman's life by taking her weapons away from her," Duke said. "And it's within the law. Whatever she's got cooking inside her will wear down and she'll cool off."

"You wanna do it?" the sheriff said with a sly grin. "If you do, I'll deputize you right now."

"Sure, anything to save a lady from a scalping. Gimme a star."

"Raise your right hand . . ."

Sheriff Mishcorte and Duke walked down towards the boardinghouse but got no farther than the grocery store. Sarah stood before the counter buying sugar and coffee. Several men stood around looking at her, listening to her talk to the storekeeper. Duke and Mishcorte pushed in the door. Mishcorte nodded to the others and winked, indicating something was about to take place with Sarah. The room quieted down as they approached.

"Ma'am," Duke said.

Sarah turned, looked at Duke and past him to the grinning sheriff. "What is it?"

"There's a town law that says nothing but law officers can carry guns."

"What about the others?" Sarah said, indicating the men standing around in back of her. "And yourself."

"I'm a deputy, ma'am. I'm asking you kindly for your gun."

"All right," Sarah said simply. "Here it is—" She drew it out and cocked it. "Take it." The movement to her hip had been so fast neither of the men had seen it. "Aren't you disarming me, Deputy?" Sarah said.

Duke's ears turned a bright red. "Ma'am, you wouldn't shoot me, not in front of all these witnesses. And—you oughtta be careful—"

Sarah took his hat off, then fired on the floor, fanning the gun expertly. Duke scrambled for his hat and danced wildly to escape the bullets. Sarah put the gun away. "Want to try again, Deputy?" she said coldly. "Any time."

She gathered her bags together, put a double eagle on the counter and waited for her change. "Those Comanches were north of here, did you say?"

Duke nodded.

At the door, Sarah stopped and addressed all of them. "My father was a colonel in the Confederate Army. I cut my baby teeth on the barrel of a dueling pistol." She closed the door.

Behind her she could hear them burst into laughter. She smiled a little to herself. She had hated to put the young cowboy to shame before the others; she knew he was only trying to help her. The corners of her mouth came down in a straight line. Nothing was going to help until she discovered a tall Indian named One Nest.

CHAPTER FIVE

SARAH rode out of Lister as the first streaks of dawn were breaking the eastern barriers. She snapped the roan hard on the flanks and pointed north. She did not look back or to either side as she bent to the big trail.

She had ridden hard for several hours and was out in the wild, flat country, now dry and wasted from greenness to sand and desert. It was hard country and the sun was hot. She dropped from the roan near a little stream that was still high from the heavy spring thaws, and refilled her canteen. It was then that she saw the lone rider coming up after her.

She pulled the carbine down from the roan's flap and settled herself behind a small clump of brush. When the rider was within range, she pulled down once and saw the dust kick high before the black animal's forelegs. The rider pulled up sharply.

"It's me, ma'am—" a voice carried to her. "Gibson Duke!"

Sarah recognized the rider then. She came up behind the bush and held the carbine high. She waved him in, but did not let him get from her sights. Duke moved in slowly and cautiously. "Ma'am, I remembered something about them Comanche that I forgot to tell you—"

"What is it?" she demanded. The carbine had him dead-center.

"Well, if you'd let me get off and rest a bit, and get some water for my animal, I'd tell you. Gladly."

"Tell me from there," Sarah said coldly.

"Don't be unfriendly, ma'am," he said. "You could drop me the minute I made a wrong move. But you set a mighty pace. I'm tuckered."

Sarah hesitated. "All right," she said moving away from the stream. She whistled for the roan, and mounted the animal when he came to her. Sitting in the saddle, she nodded. "You can git down now, mister."

"You shore don't take no chances, do you?" Duke grinned easily. He let the black go to the water, and ducked his own head beneath the surface. He came up dripping. "Ma'am, them Comanche I told you about—they just come back from a little fight they had with some other Injuns—Apache I think—leastwise the hair they had on the scalp sticks looked full and black. And from the looks of the village, when I passed, they didn't want no company. They musta lost a few of their braves, and they ain't got over worrying about it yet. It might be dangerous for you to just ride in—"

"You said all that last night," Sarah said, bringing up the carbine. "Now look, Mr. Duke, I've got something I have to do, and you nor anyone else is going to stop me. I don't need help—don't want any—" She paused and her voice grated. "And I don't want no man."

Duke shook his head. "I understand, ma'am," he said. "But I sure hate to see you—"

"Why!" demanded Sarah. She nudged the roan closer to the man. "Why do you hate to see me go?"

"I took a shine to you," Duke said. "And that's no lie, I'm telling you. I don't know what you've got on for them Comanche, or what—"

"Didn't you see the wedding ring?" Sarah said, extending her hand.

"Yessum. I sure did. But then I figured there wasn't no more husband, leastwise not much of one if he let you roam around looking like a saddlebum hunting down Injuns."

"That's what you figured?"

"Yessum."

"All right, you've said your piece. Now climb back on the black and git. If I see you again, mister, I'll shoot you down like a rattlesnake. There was only one man—and he's dead. I ain't after no other."

Duke nodded. He looked her straight in the eye. "All right, Miss Sarah."

"How did you know my name?" she demanded.

"Boardinghouse lady told me." Duke climbed back into the saddle of the black. "I hope you took everything I said to you right, Miss Sarah. I mean it. Whatever your trouble, I'd like to help you with it."

"Nobody can help," Sarah said, turning to look over the stream. She lowered the carbine and slipped it into the sheath. "I understand and appreciate what you said to me, but there's something I've got a calling to do alone."

She snapped the pony around and sent the roan splashing through the stream. She did not look back at the rider who sat watching her, tall in the saddle.

"Horse," Duke said to the animal, "we been traveling together come six years soon. That there woman is in deep trouble, down in her innards. And she's a hell of a woman for any man. Now, I just ain't lucky enough to run across two women like that in one lifetime. We ain't never backed down from a fight before, and this'n looks as good as I've seen."

Duke rolled a cigarette and raised one leg over the pommel of his saddle. He smoked slowly, and when he was finished, he wheeled the black into the stream and began slowly trotting after Sarah Phelps.

The spread of tipi was snug down tight against a full stream that had backwatered up onto the grass—a dozen skin tents. Like a mirror, in the backwater's smooth surface reflected the colors and the triangles of the lodges. Down near the water, Sarah could see the horses, several younger bucks attending them. The squaws moved in and out of their tipi and worked over fires. There was no sign of the other braves, but she knew they were not far away. She counted more than thirty horses nuzzling the sweetwater grass and drinking the clear water.

She waited, head down in the grass, with just a few blades parted for her to see, for One Nest to appear. She wanted to learn which tent was his, she wanted to find out if he had children, she wanted to find out as much about the Comanche chief as possible before she decided what she would do.

Night fell slowly, enveloping the sky in the fold of a midnight blue blanket. She did not move. She had left the roan a mile behind her in a stand of cottonwood trees and worked her way up to the village slowly and carefully.

She sipped the water from her canteen and waited.

There were only the lights from inside the tipi and the dying fires before the lodges now. She had seen no one that resembled One Nest, but she knew he was there. Well after the last of the fires before the tipi had gone out, she moved out slowly. She had spotted the chief's lodge from the size of it and the activity around it. The bucks entered slowly and came out fast. There was no other lodge that could be the chief's. She pulled the carbine up close to her side and worked her way silently down to the edge of the village, ears straining for the slightest noise. She made the opposite side of the tipi and waited.

There was a cry from the area where the horses were and she froze, but settled down when she realized it was only the young bucks cavorting around. Someone inside of the tipi she had decided belonged to One Nest spoke loudly and harshly.

Sarah waited, forcing herself to wait a full five minutes, counting off the time slowly to make sure, and then she moved. Quickly, bent over low, she made the side of the tipi and listened. There were sounds inside, strange sounds of half-talk, half-chant. She clenched her teeth and worked her way around to the front of the tent, took a deep breath and leaped in.

The carbine up, she stopped short. She saw three very old Indians, dressed in fine skins, scraped and bleached to whiteness, with beautiful feathered headworks and painted faces. They looked up at her, startled.

They all began to shout at once. Sarah became confused. Neither of the men before her was One Nest. She backed up—and then felt the steel grip of an arm around her neck. She dropped the carbine and began tearing at the arm.

There was an explosion, the arm relaxed and she knew she had been saved.

The three old men were reaching for her. There was another explosion—then another and a third.

"Grab your gun and let's get outa here," Duke said to her.

Still confused, Sarah grabbed the carbine and raced after the tall cowboy blindly. Behind her she could hear the shouts and cries of the entire village, but she did not stop to look around. Stumbling, falling, she followed the retreating figure of Gibson Duke into the cottonwood trees below the village and into the water. "I've got our horses on the other side of the stream." Duke said. "Sarah, I hope to God you know how to swim."

Sarah plunged into the icy stream without answering,

struggling with the carbine, thrashing her way across to the other side. She pulled herself up out of the water a few yards ahead of Duke.

"This way!" he said and sloshed past her into a thicket. Sarah stumbled and dove headlong into a clump of brush. Duke's hands went around her thin waist and lifted her up bodily and ran through the thicket. The black and the roan waited silently.

"Quick!" he said. "They still don't know what hit 'em."

They climbed into the saddles and beat their way out of the thicket and began pounding hard across the flats.

They broke around the corner of a small butte and suddenly Duke pulled up on the black and pointed to what apparently was a sheer height of wall. He posted his black hard up the dry ledges of the butte with Sarah on the roan a few yards behind him.

"In here!" he shouted. He moved through a thin narrow pass that was not visible from below, rounded the inner walls and came out into a huge hollow. "We'll see which way they go from here," Duke said to her. "Then if they go on ahead across the plains after us, we can sneak out the back way, double in back of the village and make it the hell out of the whole district."

Suddenly there was the distant pounding of hoofs. It sounded like hundreds of them. Duke braced himself and climbed up the side of the hollow. He squinted down through an opening that gave him a view of the horizon and the flats for miles. The entire village of braves was strung out below the butte, heading for the plains.

He slipped down. "All right; this way."

Leading their ponies, Duke moved through the hollow and slipped through another pass as small as the first one. They emerged from the center of the butte that overlooked the village, and, further, to the dryness of the flats north of Lister.

"Let's go!" he said.

They climbed into the saddle and hurried their nervous horses down the steep decline to the hard-packed floor of the flats, struck straight west and well beyond the Comanche village, and disappeared into the thick brush country of the Panhandle flats.

They rode hard all night, stopping only when they knew their ponies would drop beneath them.

Duke pulled up beneath a grove of cottonwood and brush and slipped to the ground. The sun was up and their faces were smeared with sweat and grime. Sarah collapsed on the ground, sinking her head into her arms. Duke slipped the saddles off the horses and left them where they lay.

He slipped to the ground, put his head on one of the blanket rolls and was asleep in a minute.

Sarah awoke to the smell of coffee. It was close on to dark, and she rubbed her eyes. "Oh," she said softly, not looking at Duke. "I remember now."

"Coffee's ready in a minute," Duke said gently. "You wanna wash your face, Miss Sarah? There's a canteen over there."

Sarah nodded and poured a palmful of water into her hands. She wiped most of the grime off with her neckerchief and came back to the edge of the fire and sat down.

They drank coffee and ate bacon and sourdough bread hungrily. "What was you aiming to do in the medicine tent, ma'am?" Duke asked softly.

"Was that what it was?"

"If they'd of caught us. I reckon they'd of turned us over on a spit like a roastin' jackrabbit on the trail."

"I thought it was the chief's tipi," she said. "I saw everyone going in and out."

"They was probably moaning over losing some of their braves in that fight they just had."

Sarah nodded, but kept her eyes averted.

"You didn't tell me what you was aiming to do, Miss Sarah."

"No, I didn't."

Duke put a piece of wood on the fire and kicked up the falling embers. "You don't have to tell me, ma'am."

Sarah was silent.

"I declared myself back at the watering stream, ma'am, and I'm sticking by what I said."

Sarah looked up. "And I told you I didn't want, or need a man." Her voice was cold, but not biting. "Why did you follow me?"

It was Duke's turn to keep his eyes on the fire.

"It isn't going to do you any good, Mr. Duke," Sarah said, a trace of softness creeping into her voice. "There's something I've got to do—and there ain't enough time in the world for anything but my promise."

"Promise to who, ma'am?"

"Never mind. But I want you to know I appreciate what you did back there," Sarah said. "I thought that medicine tent was old One Nest's tipi."

Duke frowned. "One nest? What's that?"

"Name of a Comanche I'm looking for."

Duke shook his head. "I thought I told you back in Lister, Miss Sarah, this here bunch is old Kaygeesee's tribe. Part of them anyway." He paused. "I can't rightly say I ever heard of a Comanche named One Nest."

Sarah sipped her coffee and did not reply.

"Are you sure he's a chief?" Duke asked.

"Yes."

"From around these parts?"

Sarah threw the dregs out of her cup and refilled it with the simmering coffee. "You don't seem to know much about Comanche, Mr. Duke. Comanche don't come from any particular part of Texas. They're from all over, and they move around a lot."

"I reckon I know that, ma'am," Duke said quietly. "But old chief Kaygeesee has been in the watershed area of the Brazos for quite a few years. He was here even before I went up north."

"It's possible, isn't it," Sarah said, "that the Injun I'm looking for could be part of Kaygeesee's tribe? Splintered off from the main nation, in a way?"

"Yessum, that's a possibility. But the sheriff back in Lister knows a lot about Injun doings and especially about Kaygeesee's outfit. Don't you reckon he would have heard of this here One Nest?"

Sarah got up and walked to her pony, examining the animal's hoofs and legs carefully. Duke watched her from across the fire and sipped his coffee.

"I wish I could make you see my point, Miss Sarah," Duke said slowly. "I want to help you. I reckon, if I have to say it, I did pull you out of a terrible hole back in that medicine tipi."

Sarah walked slowly back to the fire and stood across from the cowboy, her eyes searching his face.

Duke found it difficult to look into her face; he

glanced up once, but under the steady gaze Sarah leveled at him he dropped his eyes to the fire. "How many times do I have to say my piece, ma'am?"

"How many times do I have to tell you there isn't any room in my life for a man, or even friends or companions?" Sarah replied softly. "There's something I have to do, Mr. Duke."

"Get that Injun One Nest." Duke nodded. "I know."

"That's right. That's a tough enough thing to do as it is, and takes everything I've got to keep at it, even though I haven't been doing it very long. But I'm going to get him, Mr. Duke. I'll track that red-skinned heathen straight to hell and put a forty-five slug in his brain and help push him over the divide."

"But why, Miss Sarah?" Duke asked softly.

"It isn't important that I tell you, Mr. Duke. Only thing that's important is that I got to do it."

Sarah turned away from the fire and walked away into the darkness.

Duke sat alone, sipping his coffee, and when after an hour Sarah had not returned, he slipped off his boots and stretched out on his blanket roll. He did not go to sleep right away. He lay awake until he heard her return and settle down on the other side of the fire.

It was about midnight that Duke saw Sarah get up quietly and pull on her boots. She saddled the roan, speaking softly to the animal and looking back over her shoulder at the prone figure of Duke. She stood a moment, looking down at him, mounted and then whirled the pony around and slipped quietly away from the dying light of the fire.

She was out of sound and sight when Duke moved. He hurried to his horse, saddled, gathered his blanket and gear, kicked the fire out and trailed out after her.

Duke trailed her all night, keeping just in earshot of her softly walking roan. When the sun began to break the east, he saw the slumping figure of Sarah sleeping in the saddle.

He spurred the black and rode up beside her. Sarah did not even wake up. Duke grinned, reached over and took hold of the reins that dangled loose and led the pony, glancing now and then at Sarah to see if she was all right.

Sarah did not wake up until the sun was high. She pulled up straight and looked around, startled, and then she saw Duke.

"Ready for some coffee, Miss Sarah?" Duke said.

Sarah stared at him a long time, her face swollen just a bit from the heavy sleeping. She nodded slightly and slipped from the pony.

"Here's plenty of water, Miss Sarah, if you'd like to wash the sleep out of your eyes." Duke said, handing over an oversized canteen of water. "I'll make a fire and fixing's over there beyond that clump of brush and you'll have all the privacy you need, ma'am."

Duke stood holding the leather of the two horses, smiling softly at her, squinting against the morning sun.

"All right, Mr. Duke," Sarah said. "I guess I could use a wash."

For the first time, Sarah smiled at the sunburned Westerner. She walked a few steps, stopped suddenly and turned back to him. "Put a pinch of salt in your coffee water, Mr. Duke; it'll make a difference in the taste."

Duke's face broke out into a smile. "Yes, ma'am. I'll do that."

They had finished eating sourdough bread and drank nearly all of the coffee when Duke turned to her and broke the silence. "Miss Sarah, if you'd tell me about this Injun, I might know something that would help us."

"First, there's some things that have to be straightened out between us, Mr. Duke," Sarah said.

Duke's face sobered. "All right, ma'am."

"I didn't ask for your help."

"That's true, right enough."

"In fact I tried to avoid your help on three different occasions."

"Yessum."

"I don't want no man—and the first time you make a move toward me that isn't proper and that I judge fitting, I'll kill you where you stand."

Duke's eyes flinched and steadied. "Yes, ma'am," he said softly.

"I got me something I have to do—catch and kill that Injun."

"Going to tell me what he done?"

Sarah was quiet a long time. "He killed my husband, who was a fine man. I reckon anybody that would come out to this crazy country has a right to expect that from the Injuns, in a way.'

"Yes, ma'am."

"But that ain't all. He killed my children. A little boy—he scalped the boy—and he—violated my little girl." Sarah's faced hardened. "The girl was just a little thing."

"Yes, ma'am." Duke said.

"We had given him beef to eat when he was hungry and we treated him right, because my husband was a fair-minded man, and then he came back and killed him." Sarah's voice was strong, but she could not look at Duke. "I say that killing my husband was one thing that coulda been understood. This is a hard country, and there ain't no getting around it, regardless of how you look at it, the Injuns were here first."

Duke's eyes sharpened. "That's true, Miss Sarah."

"But it's the children that I'm thinking of." She stopped. "No, not just the children, it's all of it together."

"Where you figure on looking, Miss Sarah?"

Sarah didn't answer for some time. "Everywhere, Mister Duke. Everywhere there's an Injun tipi, I'm going to look for One Nest."

"That could take a long time, ma'am. This is a big country and there's lots of Indians."

"I know it, but I told you I didn't ask for your help. I'd just as soon you left right now."

"I'll go with you, Miss Sarah."

"And you understand about how things are between us?"

"Yes, ma'am."

"And I ain't promising no rewards, or pay, or nothing for your help." Sarah looked at him squarely. "You get nothing, Mr. Duke."

"Yes, ma'am."

"You understand?"

"I understand," Duke said. He stood up. "Where you want to start looking first, Miss Sarah?"

"Since it's spring," Sarah said, standing up beside him, "I figure they might be following the buffalo north. We'll track after the Texas herd up through the Panhandle and into Kansas and Colorado."

"That sounds reasonable," Duke replied.

"Let's go, then." Sarah said.

"Yes, ma'am."

They kicked out the fire and pulled into saddle. They pointed their ponies to the north, with the rising eastern sun burning their faces though the dew was still fresh on the grass and brush. They were in no hurry. The horses walked and their eyes searched the horizons for signs of dust and movement. At noon, they removed their winter slickers and coats and Duke saw for the first time the slim, hard outlines of Sarah's shoulders and waist. His eyes traveled to the high, mature breasts beneath the man's shirt and turned away. He spurred his pony and the black leaped ahead a few paces and he stared right into the sun, as if to burn out the picture of what he had seen.

CHAPTER SIX

THEY MOVED up the buffalo line, always pointing north, never too busy to scout a fire or smoke trail or take the time to surround and carefully survey a stand of tipi, regardless of what kind of Indian village it might be. When it rained and the ponies were knuckle-deep in mud, they made a smouldering fire and hunched beneath their slickers and blankets. When the sun was burning hot and the first of the summer dusters bore down out of the northern plains, Duke would ride several hundred yards ahead of Sarah while she stripped down and cooled off.

Duke did most of the meat making, riding off sometimes half the day and out of gunshot sound of Sarah, to return with a brace of jack rabbits, or a deer, or some sort of fowl. When they hit water, they stopped and rested their horses and washed their clothes and rested.

Sarah did not talk much. She accepted cooking and fire-making and water-gathering and the collecting of wood as part of her chores. Duke in turn hunted for them, stood night sentry, catnapping during the day as they rode, or when he could; he cared for the horses, and once when they caught a small deer and trailed it after them when they began to hit the desolate regions between the North Wichita River and the Red River, it was Sarah who finally had to put a forty-five slug in the animal's head. Duke stoutly refused, saying that he had already become fond of the animal; even after Sarah did shoot it, he wouldn't eat any of it. Sarah said nothing and let him eat sourdough for three days and only smiled when he finally shamefacedly tore into a roasting cut of the venison.

Conversation between the two was simple and direct, mostly calling one or the other's attention to some chore to be done, or to lend a hand, or to take a look at the dust trail ahead of them and speculate on its origins. They moved almost lazily through the early days of summer, always pointing north and following the buffalo and searching constantly for signs of Indians, particularly Comanches.

They had ridden for nearly five weeks without seeing another white person when they topped a rise in the northern stretches above the Big Red close on to the Canadian River and saw the slow developing spine of a cattle drive out of New Mexico.

Duke squinted at the riders at the point. One of the men rode a pinto. He nodded in its direction. "If I'm right, that hardtail on the calico pony is a friend from the other side."

Sarah's eyes studied the figure. "Other side of what?"

Duke hesitated. "The law, Miss Sarah."

"Have you ever been on the other side, Mr. Duke?" she asked carefully.

"I reckon some people might care to call it that. It was only a case of gettin' or being got by a no-account."

"Did that rider on the pinto figure in it?"

"If it's the one I think it is, ma'am."

Sarah hesitated a moment. "They could tell us a thing or two," she said finally. "If they've seen anything along the trail of our Indian."

"Yes ma,'am" Duke's face was hard.

"You got a special reason for not wanting to see your friend?"

"If you want to go ask 'em, Miss Sarah, we'll go ask."

"But you don't want to, is that it?"

"I ain't even sure it's the same fellow."

Sarah's eyes searched her companion's face. "Ain't afraid, are you?"

Duke's face reddened. He turned slowly and looked Sarah in the eye. "Ma'am, I ain't afraid of anything that walks or crawls on God's green earth. If you want to go down asking questions, I'll lead the way." He whipped his pony around hard and dropped down the slow rise, kicking up dust as Sarah followed.

The outriders and the men on point stopped their pony and turned to meet the two riders coming in on them from the south.

Duke had gained a few hundred yards on Sarah and pulled up short and stood still before the half-dozen cowmen. Sarah drew up alongside and jerked back on the leather, a little excited and breathless over the prospect of getting information about One Nest.

The rider on the pinto held a carbine pointed at them. He nudged his pony forward and walked the few remaining yards that separated them. He was a tall, rangy man, burned brown from the sun and covered from hat to boot with red dust. "Whoa up, pony!" he said softly. "Well, bad penny, hey Duke? How you been?" The other riders drew up behind him and studied the newcomers.

Duke nodded. "Hello, Barb. I been fine, I reckon."

Barb's eyes flicked over to Sarah. "Howdy, ma'am. Excuse me for not being overpolite, but your husband and me ain't seen eye to eye over a couple of things in the past."

"He's not my husband," Sarah said.

Barb's head nodded gently. "Yes, ma'am." He continued to look at Duke. "Son, how come you ride in on me like this? You could have spotted my pony and figured it was a New Mexico herd and that it might be me." He shook his head again. "Careless, Duke."

Gibson Duke had not moved a muscle. "Miss Sarah has a few questions to ask you."

"That's how come, huh?"

Duke was silent.

"Ask your questions, ma'am," Barb said. "I might not be able to answer 'em after a while. Ain't that right, Duke?"

"I'm looking for a Comanch' chief. One Nest is what he calls himself. He's got big hands, a thick nose and he's tall."

"Sounds like most any Comanche, ma'am." Barb said.

"Have you seen him?" Duke asked harshly.

"Hey, you talk tough for a man that's about to lose his lights and liver to the buzzards." The men behind Barb laughed.

"Would you shoot me—right here—without facing me?"

"Why, sure," Barb said. "But to answer the lady's question, Duke, we ain't seen nothing but a few lonesome-looking Apaches looking hungrily after some of our critters."

"Have you heard any talk about him?" Sarah asked.

"No, we ain't, ma'am." He turned his head slightly. "Have any of you boys heard about a Comanche named One Nest, with a fat nose and big hands?"

There was a chorus of *no's* from the men.

Duke nodded toward the herd. "I see you finally rustled enough critters for a drive, Barb. Wouldn't it be easier to rob a bank and steal cash, instead of driving cattle through Indian country?"

Barb's eyes sharpened. "Duke, damn it, you just insist on talking out, don't you?"

"I say what I please. I told Jasper that too. And he didn't like it."

"Like me. I don't like it."

"Jasper tried to draw."

"And I ain't trying. I got you, Duke, and I'm going to kill you."

Duke spoke to Sarah. "Miss Sarah, you might as well know. I wouldn't trust this rustler as far as I could spit. He might kill me and tell you a whacked-up story about me that ain't true."

"All right, Duke, you tell her."

"I killed his brother. I accused him of stealing cattle before witnesses and he drew on me and I killed him."

"Only the lawman back in Sante Fe thinks you didn't give him a chance to draw," Barb said.

"After you threatened him," Duke said quietly, "he changed his mind."

Barb shrugged. "I'm sorry to leave you stranded like this, ma'am, killing off your man, but you're welcome to tag along with us if you want to." Barb raised the carbine.

There was the explosive roar of a Colt and Barb dropped the carbine and grabbed his arm. Sarah held the Colt level and steady. "Better move out, Mr. Duke. I'll be along after you."

Barb grimaced with pain, but he managed to grin. "Damn it, ma'am, you most shattered the bone in my arm. Pretty good shooting."

"I can just as easily put one through your head, or any of you others that tries to prevent us from leaving."

"We ain't going to try nothing, ma'am." said one of the nearest of the men. "But it don't seem right riding off without them two coming to a settlement."

Sarah's eyes flashed. "Would you have stopped him from killing Mr. Duke in cold blood?"

None of them replied.

"Let's go, Mr. Duke," Sarah said.

Duke grinned at Sarah. "Thank you, Miss Sarah, but I can't ride out of here without settling something one way or the other with him."

"Don't be stupid," Sarah said, her face growing hot with impatience and outrage. "He tried to kill you in cold blood."

"That's his way, ma'am. He don't know no better."

Sarah tossed her head angrily. "You're coming along with me."

"No, I ain't," Duke said.

Barb and the others began to grin. Sarah looked at them and moved her pony alongside of Duke. She made a motion with her hands as if she were going to plead with him and then quickly brought the barrel of the gun down on Duke's head. The man slumped forward in his saddle and nearly sagged out. Sarah grabbed his shirt and held him up, pulled at the reins and whirled the two ponies around, twisting her body as she did to keep the others covered wih the Colt. "This is the way it's going to be," she said, steely-voiced. She fired quickly and took Barb's hat off at the hair line, wheeled and fired again, taking the hat off another. "I'll shoot to kill the first man that follows us."

She nudged her pony and led the unconscious Duke away from the startled group of men. Five hundred yards away, Sarah heard them begin to laugh. She topped a rise and dropped into a brush on the other side, moved more quickly in the dense thickets, and rode that way for an hour before she broke free of the brush and pulled to a stop in a little clearing. She slipped off her pony, hurried to Duke's side and eased him gently to the ground. She hesitated, and then, making her decision, tied the Westerner hand and foot, removed his Colt and belt and led his pony away to grass.

Satisfied Duke would remain still, she left the brush and circled back to check the cattle drive. She watched the men from several different positions the rest of the afternoon before she was satisfied they were not going to trail after Duke and herself, turned her roan back toward the brush and what she knew would be a furious, outraged man.

As Sarah walked the roan back toward the brush, she smiled to herself. Things change rapidly in this wild country, she thought. For a moment she allowed her thoughts to drift back to the rolling green hills of Georgia and her home and the way of life before the war. There was a moment when the sun was fading fast, dropping beyond the red flats of New Mexico, that Sarah Phelps stopped the roan and stared at the redness and remembered evenings when her father would come in from the fields and overseeing of the slaves in the huge plantation. At this time of day she would sit on his lap while he drank his coffee black and strong and tell him about the things she had done while he was away. Then when the sun would begin to fade to the west, they would grow silent and watch the fields grow purplish as the sun turned blood-red, and they'd listen to the lovely little night sounds.

She listened for the night sounds now as she moved back toward the brush and the bound Gibson Duke. She heard the ferrets coming out of their holes and she could hear the call of some animal mother to its young—and in the distance she could hear the lowing of the cattle in the drive as they settled for the night. And suddenly there was a screech and hoot of an owl—

Sarah Phelps stiffened in the saddle. She moved her head slowly and studied the brush that was on her right side and somewhat ahead of her. She spoke casually to the roan. "Tired, I'll bet, aren't you, pony. Well, soon now you'll have your grass and a cool drink—and I'll see if I can't get Mr. Duke to give you a little brushing down. You're beginning to look a sight."

But even as she spoke, her ears were tuned to the screeching hoot of that owl again. There was something about it that was not quite right somehow.

She moved on steadily, slipping forward a little in the saddle to pretend a close examination of the reins, actually cutting her eyes sideways into the brush looking for movement or shadows or for the screech of the owl again, hoping to locate its position.

She straightened up and suddenly she saw the flash of a naked arm in the brush.

Sarah didn't wait. She heeled the roan around hard, jerked the Colt out of her holster and charged at a full gallop toward the spot where she had seen the flash of naked skin. Ten feet from the wall of brush, she pulled hard on the leather and the roan skidded to a stop, the dust still flying as Sarah charged into the thicket, moving low and fast, her eyes searching, Colt high and ready.

She fired deep to her right, and dropped to the ground. She remained still. There was another movement in the same direction. She fired again, snapping it off quickly.

"Eeee-yaaaa!"

Sarah got up and charged into the brush. The Indian lay on the ground holding his chest, thick streams of blood spurting through his fingers. He stared up at Sarah, then closed his eyes and sank to the ground.

Sarah glanced around, and, seeing nothing move, eased toward the dead Indian. It was a Comanche, all right, but there was no way of telling where he had come from. Probably out making meat, she thought. If that were true, then there must be a pony around somewhere. Without another glance at the dead man, she slipped deeper into the brush, all the time searching for movement, alert for the slightest sound.

Sarah stopped near a stunted oak tree and listened. She moved on a little further, eyes continually searching and ears tuned to the noise of the underbrush. Then she spotted a clearing a few yards to her right. She moved toward it cautiously.

The clearing was empty—except for two bareback Indian ponies.

They raised their heads and looked at her and then continued to nuzzle the grass. Sarah stopped and searched around her. She would have to move fast. It was growing dark and she had to get back to Duke.

She backtracked to the edge of the brush, skirting the dead Indian's position, but careful to come close enough to it to see if there was any movement around it. She broke clear of the brush and looked for her roan.

The sun was full down now; not even the red hues

of a few minutes before were left. The sky was dead white and darkening perceptibly toward the east. She moved into the open, glancing over her shoulder to cover her retreat from the protective brush, and searched for the roan. She found the animal grazing contentedly over the first rise and slipped into the saddle, whirled around and drove the pony hard toward the clearing and Gibson Duke. If there were two braves, and the other had heard the shot that Sarah had killed the first with, Duke might be in trouble.

Even as she rode, Sarah Phelps was acutely aware that she had grown fond of Gibson Duke. Fleetingly she wondered about how fickle emotions were that could force the memory of her husband and her children back out of her mind, even for a moment.

It was full dark when Sarah dropped from the roan and worked her way carefully into the brush where she had left Gibson Duke tied hand and foot, unable to defend himself if the rider of the second Indian pony discovered him.

She moved fast, but silently, broke through the opening and breathed easier. Duke glared up at her in the darkness when she approached him, bending over to untie his hands. "It's about time you showed up—Miss Sarah!" His voice was angry, but restrained.

"Shh!" she warned. "We have company."

"Barb?"

"Injuns. I just plucked one of 'em, but there were two of the red devils in this brush. You heard anything?"

Duke shook his head and with his hands free, began to untie his legs. His anger faded almost immediately. He picked up his gun and checked it. "Are you sure there's two of them?"

"I found two horses."

"Who were they?"

"Comanches," Sarah replied.

They waited in the still darkness, back to back, facing out, Colts high and ready. "I want you to know, Miss Sarah," Duke whispered over his shoulder, "that I thank you for saving my hide from that skunk, but I don't rightly know how to feel about you clobbering me over the head and taking me out of a fight."

"Shut up!" Sarah hissed. "I think I heard something."

"Over to your right," Duke replied. "Circle around, and come up in back. Shoot first and don't worry about hitting me."

Sarah moved away with a nod that Duke could not see and hit the first clump of brush quietly. She listened and heard Duke, opposite her, making another circle. There was a slight sound, like the first, as if someone were turning over in dry leaves, straight ahead of her. She inched forward, breathing tightly, pushing along the ground with her free hand and lifting her body clear of the tangled brush.

She saw the Indian's head and the movement the same instant she heard the *thung!* of the bowstring. She dropped to the ground and fired.

She emptied the Colt after the slight movement and where she thought the Indian would be.

Suddenly there was a wild crashing noise opposite her. Duke came thundering through the brush, bellowing at the top of his voice. "Miss Sarah—Miss Sarah! Are you hurt?"

There was a cry, followed by a scuffle. A shot was squeezed off. Then silence.

Sarah waited. It seemed an eternity before she heard movement in the brush. Duke came toward her. "You can come out now, Miss Sarah," he said.

Sarah found the Indian sprawled on the ground, covered with blood. "You hit him four times," Duke said.

"I'm sorry," Sarah said quietly. "That makes two I killed."

"It was them or us, ma'am," Duke said.

"I know."

"And I figure you're going to have to kill some more if you go on with this hunt for your Injun chief."

"Don't try to talk me out of it, Mr. Duke."

"No, ma'am. Just telling you how things are going to be."

"I know how things are going to be."

They drank coffee and pulled at deer meat and stared into the small fire. "They probably come from around here somewhere," Duke said after a long period of silence.

"I guess they do."

"It won't be safe to hang around in this brush much

longer. When these two don't show up, they might send others to look for them."

"And suppose it's One Nest's village?" Sarah said.

"That's a likelihood, ma'am."

"Then instead of running away from them, Mr. Duke, I'm going to look for their village."

"I was afraid you'd say that."

Sarah stood up. "I guess the score is kind of even, Mr. Duke, if that's the way you feel."

"Feeling no way in particular, Miss Sarah."

"You saved my bacon from the medicine lodge and I returned the favor with that calico rider named Barb. We can call it quits right now, if you have a mind to," Sarah said slowly.

Duke shook his head in protest. "Damn it, woman, I didn't say I was going to walk out."

"Then stop trying to get me to quit! Tell me one thing, Mr. Duke. What am I going to do if I do quit?"

"What are you going to do when you find him—and get him, if you're that lucky?"

"I'll think about that when the time's here," Sarah said. "I'm riding, Mr. Duke."

She got up and moved to the roan, swung into the saddle and waited while Duke kicked out the fire and signaled to his black. They moved out of the brush and stopped at the edge, staring out over the dark, unfolding flatlands.

"Since this is still early summer," Duke said, "it's a possibility that these two came from a village up the trail to the north."

"What makes you think so?"

"How many bluffer have we seen in the last two weeks?"

"Not many."

"Neither has anybody else." Duke said. "And that includes the Injuns. It ain't reasonable they would be out making meat for little game in the brush like this, if they had plenty of bluffer meat at hand."

Sarah nodded. "Trailing after the bluffer, and not finding any, they would double back into this brush for meat."

Without a word, she heeled the roan around and pointed it north across the flats at a slow gallop.

A little after midnight they pulled to stop before a stand of half a dozen tipi. The cookfires were out, but there was still the smarting red glow of embers in the dark earth.

"Not a very big village," Duke said quietly.

The hot desert winds had chilled off during the night and they both pulled at their brush jackets. "We can sit and wait for 'em to come out and see if your Injun is here, or we can ride in and roust 'em out. They won't do a hell of a lot of fighting if we surprise them."

"That means taking care of their guards," Sarah replied.

"Well, yes, ma'am. We'd have to do that first."

"And if we wait for 'em to show up, they might catch wind of us and go to wondering about their meat-making party that didn't come back yet."

"All them things is logical," Duke said.

Sarah Phelps turned in her saddle and faced her companion. "If you got anything on your mind, Mr. Duke, I would just as soon you come right out with it."

Duke wagged his head and kept silent.

"Well?" Sarah demanded. "You still fretting about the way I handled you back there with them cowmen?"

Duke kept his silence.

"There wasn't no other way—"

Duke cut her off. "Yes, there was, Miss Sarah," he said gently. "I reckon I could of slipped my saddle and put a wad in old Barb's head before he could pull the trigger."

Sarah humphed. "I don't know about gun fighting, Mr. Duke, but it seems to me that when a man has a carbine leveled at your head—a man intent on killing you—there isn't much you can do. I always heard you don't make a move if another fellow's got the drop on you."

Duke nodded heavily. "That's true, ma'am, but that rule is like any other kinda rule or saying. It lulls men into overconfidence. Now take old Barb. He's a tough one, all right, in more ways than one, and knows a lot about handling guns and all, and he knows about not drawing against a man who has the drop on you, and that's just what I was counting on."

"It sounds as if you was messing around with losing a head if you ask me."

"Well, Miss Sarah, I didn't ask you."

"Well, you're here, ain't you? And no blood shed, either."

"I'm here," he said.

"If you'd have got that Barb, them others would've gunned you down like a rattler."

"That may have been the case."

"And me along with it."

Duke was silent.

"And nothing is going to stop me from getting that Injun," Sarah said with finality.

"Well, ma'am," Duke said, and his voice was edged in a manner that Sarah had not heard before, "be careful how you put me down before other gents. I reckon I can take a lot of things and understand a heap more, but I don't fancy to having me taken by a woman pulling me out of fights."

Sarah opened her mouth to speak and then clapped her lips closed and pressed them tightly. Whatever she thought of Gibson Duke, or any other man for that matter, she knew that where a man's pride was concerned, she had better tread carefully.

"I'm sorry about that, Mr. Duke. And I promise you I won't interfere in your private affairs again."

She heard Gibson Duke let out a deep breath, without haste. She glanced at his profile in the darkness, barely making out the sharp lines of his nose and chin beneath the wide-brimmed hat.

"Be still!" Duke hissed. "Don't try for your gun!"

A dozen braves moved around them in a circle, bowstrings tight and leveled, a few carbines held high.

"Don't move and don't raise your hands," Duke whispered. "But watch me—follow my lead."

Sarah stiffened, turning her head slowly to watch the Indians move in closer and draw the circle trap tighter around them.

Two braves lowered their guns and snatched the leather out of their hands, jerking the horses. Suddenly, both Duke and Sarah's hands were grabbed from behind and lashed quickly and expertly from behind. A guttural voice spoke an order from the darkness and the horses were led down toward the silent village.

CHAPTER SEVEN

IN THE VILLAGE the squaws came out of the tipis to watch as they were brought in and pulled from the horses. Roughly and brutally, they were dragged from the mounts and thrown into a tipi and were followed by at least two dozen men, women and children. They sat on the hard dirt floor and looked up at the sweating, greasy faces of their captors, flames from several torches lighting the expressionless faces one minute and creasing them in darkness the next.

"They're waiting for someone," Duke said. "Maybe it's your boy."

"I hope it is," Sarah said.

One of the squaws stepped forward quickly and slapped Sarah viciously across the face and another stepped in and kicked her. Several others joined in and began beating her with sticks. Sarah fell back to the ground, but did not utter a sound.

Duke closed his eyes as the women began to beat Sarah with the sticks around the head. He saw one blow land mercifully on her temple and saw her body sag. At least she wouldn't feel anything else.

The men began to yammer among themselves and turn toward the opening of the tipi to make room for someone to enter. The squaws pulled back away from the bleeding Sarah and turned to the door, where a tall Indian with a full nose and huge hands stood gazing down at her. He swung his gaze toward Duke. "Why you watch village of Comanche?" he asked in broken English.

One of the braves started to speak in his ear, but the chief silenced him with a wave of his hand. "Speak, cur!" he said to Duke.

"My woman is with child," Duke lied. "I take her to the white medicine doctor. We hoped to find friends in this village."

One Nest remained silent a long time, studying Duke and the unconscious figure of Sarah. "I have seen this squaw before," he said.

Duke shook his head. "I don't think so. We come from the land beyond the mountains, on the other side of the Apache country."

"Your woman does not look as if she carries a child," One Nest said, stepping closer to Sarah and scrutinizing her figure.

"That is the trouble," Duke said.

"My eyes are not so old that they should deceive me," One Nest said heavily. "Take them—I will try and remember where I have seen this squaw before."

The others in the tipi began to protest, demanding that Duke and Sarah be killed at once, but One Nest cut them off with a curt command. He turned and left the tent. Half of the others followed. More than a dozen turned to spit on Sarah and Duke. One of the braves pulled a wicked-looking knife and made a threatening gesture toward Sarah, all the while watching Duke. The tall Westerner stared the brave in the eye and did not flinch. He knew nothing would happen to them until One Nest gave the word.

One by one the others drifted out of the tipi until there were only three old squaws who had sat down on the floor of the tipi and stared at them. Once in a while they spoke among themselves, in monosyllables, but for the most part they remained quiet and just stared.

Duke knew that Sarah would remind One Nest where he had seen her before the moment she saw him. In fact, Duke knew that her passion for revenge on the chief was so overwhelming that she would threaten and rage in fury and make any attempt at hand to get at the Indian.

Someway, they had to get out of the village before One Nest remembered Sarah, and had them killed. But what could he do as long as the three squaws sat and looked at them like three mummies?

Once, about three in the morning, One Nest came into the tipi and held a torch over Sarah's face and studied her features. He grunted and turned back to Duke. The cowman held his breath.

One Nest threw the torch down and made short chopping motions with his hands. "These eyes have seen your woman before."

"She is a kind woman," Duke said softly. "I hope that the chief of the Comanche will remember her with good thoughts."

One Nest grunted, his eyes flashing anger at his own incapacity to remember where he had seen Sarah. He turned and stomped out of the tipi.

One of the squaws got up and waddled out after him without a word.

Duke closed his eyes, falling forward gently and lay his head on the ground. He closed his eyes, but every minute or so slitted them enough to see the two old women. One of them sighed and spoke to the other. The other refused to reply. The first spoke again insistently, and pointed to Sarah. The other refused to reply. Finally the talkative one got up and waddled across the tipi in her shapeless buckskin dress and knelt down beside Sarah. With a short, stubby forefinger, she gently prodded the white woman in the stomach. She grunted, turned and nodded her head vigorously to the second.

The second squaw made a noise as if clearing her throat. The other spoke sharply in reply, then another clearing sound from the second and the first one got up from Sarah's side and stood before her friend. They began to talk, both at once, gesturing in loud voices, and making gestures. The voices became louder and louder until they were screaming at each other and pointing toward themselves and Sarah.

There was a sudden, harsh command from the outside and the women turned toward the opening, quieting immediately. The flap was pulled back and a heavy-muscled brave, well over six feet, with flat, black eyes stuck his head inside. He spoke to them sharply and grabbed one of the women by the arm and jerked her out of the tipi. Both of them scurried outside whimpering and speaking in soft, whining voices.

The brave looked around the tipi, first at the sleeping Duke and then the unconscious Sarah. He paused and walked to her side.

He stooped down beside Sarah and touched her breast cautiously. He slipped his hand inside her shirt and Duke could see him stroking the hard, flat belly. The brave said something to himself and pulled out his knife, slitting the belt and waistband of Sarah's trousers.

The white, firm belly and thighs gleamed in the flickering torchlight. The brave, squatting down beside Sarah, keened his body back and forth, mumbling to himself. He stroked Sarah gently.

Duke moved his hands and arms slowly, gently, pushing himself upright. The smouldering cottonwood torch that One Nest had thrown to the ground lay a few feet from him. He would have to shift his whole body, crawl at least two steps to reach the heavily knotted club and then back across the tipi—a distance of about ten feet—to reach the brave.

Measuring his movements carefully, he slipped one knee out and placed it carefully on the earthern floor; he followed it with the other. Then he had his hands on the end of the torch. It was much heavier than he had thought. He turned now, slowly, and studied the back of the brave.

The Indian continued to stroke Sarah's thighs and belly, talking to himself and swaying from side to side. Duke lay flat on the ground, the club held tightly in his hands, and worked his way slowly, and carefully, breathlessly, across the tipi floor.

Four feet from the Indian, he raised the club and brought it down hard on the Indian's skull. The man flopped over sideways and lay still without uttering a sound.

Duke grabbed the knife that had fallen to the ground and slit the leather thongs that bound his wrists, then slashed at those around his ankles, drawn so tight that he had felt their bite through his boots.

He turned to Sarah. For a moment he stopped and gasped at the creamy hardness of her thighs and belly. He bit down hard on his lip and slit the leather on her hands and legs. Then he moved to the front of the tent and stared out.

At that moment a brave entered the tipi and without hesitating, Duke struck with the knife. He shoved the blade into the man's chest, twisted it slightly, and felt the man slip off the end as the weight of the body sagged to the ground.

Duke pulled the dead Indian inside and turned back to Sarah. He cradled her in his arms and slapped her face gently. "Sarah—Miss Sarah! Wake up, Sarah."

Sarah was out cold.

Duke moved back to the front of the tipi and stared out. The village street was quiet. He listened for a moment, trying to find the direction of the horses.

He waited for a minute, but then began to get impatient. He glanced back at Sarah, took a deep breath and stepped out into the open street.

He moved to the back of the tipi and slit the leather covering, and then hurriedly moved down the line of tents. Past the fourth tipi, he heard the unmistakable stamping of a horse. He hurried into the darkness, bent over low and moving fast, a knife in his hand, a second stuck in his belt.

A hundred feet from the stand of tents he found the horses, and immediately saw the lone guard over them. The Indian rode his black, lounging in the saddle, appearing to be asleep. Duke made his decision quickly. He flipped the knife in his hand and set himself. It was a long throw, but it would be nearly impossible to work his way through the horses without disturbing them and bringing the brave down on him. He judged the distance, balanced the knife in his hand and let it fly. He held his breath as the blade flew through the air. There was a distant *thunk!* and the sudden gasp of the man. Against the night sky of stars, Duke saw the body slip from the saddle.

Without hesitating, he moved forward, pulled the black around and spotted the roan. His heart leaped. Somehow they had overlooked Sarah's carbine, which was still rammed into her saddle holster.

He led the two animals back down the line of tipis, keeping well away from the tents and in the darkness. At the tipi where Sarah lay unconscious, he stopped the ponies, stroked their necks and moved toward the tent.

Sarah was just beginning to stir when Duke scooped her up in his arms. She opened her eyes and started to protest.

"Shush!" he whispered. But in her semihysterical state she could not understand him.

Standing her on the ground and holding her up with one arm, he chopped her on the neck with his fist, hard. She slumped in his arms and he swept her up and half ran toward the horses.

He had to tie her into the saddle, looping a line around her body and cinching it tightly around the animal's belly. He pulled her carbine out of the saddle boot and slipped it into his own.

Mounted, he urged the animals to move, the two horses stepped off into the darkness.

They rode all night and half the next day, and still Sarah did not regain consciousness. Late the following afternoon Duke found a small box draw that had a stream running through it and a concealed exit for getting out of the other end. He pulled her down from the roan gently and bathed her head with the clear stream water, and made her as comfortable as he could. Just before dark he managed to kill a jack rabbit with a makeshift slingshot to avoid using his gun. He made a gamy-tasting gruel for Sarah.

On the second and third day Duke watched the scouts and searchers of One Nest's village out looking for them, but they did not see the box draw and the little stream—or thought it wasn't likely the man and woman would settle in such an obvious trap.

On the fourth day the Indians did not come and on the fifth, Duke scouted the area for nearly ten miles looking both for meat and signs of the Comanche. He found a small bear cub and shot it through the head, but he saw no sign of the Indians.

When he got back to the stream, Sarah was bathing her face in the running cold water. She looked up at Gibson Duke and nodded. "There doesn't seem to be very much left of Sarah Phelps you don't know about, Mr. Duke." she said. She indicated the front of her trousers where she had managed to sew them together somehow. "But I'm not asking any questions about things that—"

Duke straightened up. "Nobody touched you, Sarah." he said. "There was an Indian that stripped you down like that, but I got to him before he did anything."

Sarah nodded.

"As for me," Duke said and set about skinning the cub. "If I have you, you're going to be alive and kicking."

Sarah wiped her bruised face on the sleeve of her shirt. "What I meant, Mr. Duke," she said evenly, "was that I'm not asking any questions." She turned her head away. "If any man had a right—" she stopped.

"I might as well tell you right now, Miss Sarah," Duke said, continuing with his work on the bear cub. "That was One Nest's bunch we run into—"

Sarah whirled around, clutching her hands to her breasts, her fingers clenching slowly, tightly into a fist. "One Nest!"

"Yes, and they cleared out."

Sarah headed for the roan. Duke jumped up after her. "Where you think you're going!" he demanded.

"After him."

"With what?" Duke demanded, trying to restrain her. "We got one carbine between us and only a few shells—and you can't even stand up without getting dizzy."

Sarah tried to wrench free of his grasp. "I'm going."

Duke pulled her back. "You ain't going no place, woman. Now you listen to me. We're going to sit right here on this stream and eat and sleep and rest until you're full well again. Then we'll go after your Indian. If we have to sit here a week, we'll find them and you can have your man—but we ain't going until I say so. And I ain't going to say so until you're rested and fed and able."

Sarah relaxed.

"They'll leave a trail a mile wide now that we're fresh on them," Duke said confidently.

Sarah nodded. "All right, Mr. Duke," she said tonelessly. She wandered back to the makeshift bed of grass and brush and sank down, her strength gone. "But we'll get him, Mr. Duke."

"Yes, ma'am, that's damn sure. We'll get that Indian."

CHAPTER EIGHT

ONE NEST did not leave a trail a mile wide. Three days of rain at the end of a week, while Sarah regained her strength, wiped the traces of the Indian village from the face of the Texas Panhandle.

They rode back to the village site and scouted for miles in an ever widening circle, but after two days' searching they found nothing. Sarah dropped to the ground and sat in the shade of her roan while the animal nuzzled at the dry plains grass. Duke remained in his saddle, back to the sun, squinting into the distance.

"What do you think, Mr. Duke?" Sarah asked.

"Many things," he replied. "They coulda gone west, toward New Mexico—or on up north after buffalo." He paused. "But I don't think they would have gone much further north, ma'am. It's getting on into summer and they wouldn't go too far after bluffer for fear of running into some Cheyenne, who don't exactly cotton to Comanches."

"One thing is sure," Sarah said. "We can't go on with one gun between us."

"That's right, ma'am, and we need other things too."

"Where you reckon we are, Mr. Duke?"

Duke squinted into the distance again. "In the middle of nowhere, Miss Sarah. You could follow your nose and get to one place about as soon as you could get to another."

"Meaning?"

"Well, ma'am, it looks to me as if we're going to have a long hunt before us. And running around the way we are is just going to wear us out. There's a way of doing things like this."

"I don't have too much money, Mr. Duke." Sarah said.

"I got a little, ma'am, that's yours without asking, but even so we need lots of things. Guns are going to cost a lot, and bullets for 'em, and another carbine gun, and clothes for the winter—"

"I'll have him before the snow comes—" Sarah said quickly.

"That may be so, but you got to look at these things in their right light."

Sarah climbed wearily into her saddle. "All right, Mr. Duke, I know what you're saying. And I realize we've got to get some weapons and supplies. We might as well get on with that first."

"Yes, ma'am." Duke nodded. "I figure the best thing we could do is trail on north—we ought to hit some bluffer some time. We could invest a few dollars in a few guns and maybe do a little hide-hunting for some extra money."

"I got about three hundred and fifty dollars in gold," Sarah said.

Duke nodded. "I only got about a hundred dollars, ma'am."

"Won't that be enough to get what we need," Sarah said quickly, "without having to sidetrack and earn money?"

"Handguns are a flat hundred dollars in Dodge City, ma'am. Out here things cost a little more. And a carbine rifle will cost a little more than that. Then there's shells—and the winter gear—"

"I told you I'd have him by the snow," Sarah said shortly.

Duke nodded. "Yes, ma'am, but we better prepare just in case, don't you think, Miss Sarah?"

She did not reply. She looked back at the site where the village of the Comanches had been, and gazed on to the west. "I'll bet if we trail on toward the Apache country, we'll find him," she said, half to herself.

"With one gun, ma'am?" Duke said softly.

Sarah sighed and shook her head wearily. "All right, Mr. Duke. Yours is a cooler head than mine for the situation, I guess. How far is it to Dodge City?"

"Better'n two hundred miles."

With a last look toward the west, beyond the rise where the village of One Nest had rested, Sarah Phelps turned her eyes to the northeast. She tried to console herself that abiding by Gibson Duke's suggestions was the best thing to do for the moment. But there was still the lingering feeling of the hunter to press on— just over that next rise—and see if the hunted is not there.

They rode into the sun without talking, defeated for

the moment, allowing their horses to pick their own trails as long as the general direction was toward Dodge City.

They were just over the Kansas line when they saw the riders coming toward them in a flurry of high dust on a late afternoon in July. They pulled their horses back to a rest, shielded behind outcropping of sandy hillock and watched the men pound their leather hard and fast.

"Won't last long if they keep going like that in this weather," Duke said thoughtfully. "Unless they have to run."

"I reckon they do," Sarah said. "See yonder?" She nodded toward the east, where a second group of riders, larger than the first by more than half, pounded down after them.

"Could be some kind of law business," Duke said. "Best thing we can do is set still and watch the parade go past."

They remained hidden until the dust had settled on the trails of the two groups of riders before moving down into the open. "We ought to make Dodge City soon," Duke said. "I've a mind that what we just saw *was* law business."

It suddenly occurred to Sarah that she knew very little about the man she had ridden and fought with for weeks. And Duke's flint-hard expression when he spoke of the law—the second time she had noticed it, the first being the run-in with Barb—caused her to look at him with curious interest. "You ever have any trouble with the law, Mr. Duke?' she asked.

Duke snapped his head around. "How come you ask, ma'am?"

"You were the one that pressed yourself on me, Mr. Duke," Sarah said. "And I told you what there is to know about me, but very little has been said about you."

Duke's face hardened. "Ask your questions, then."

They rode along half a mile, fighting the sun, before Sarah spoke. "That fellow Barb—he mentioned Jasper—"

"His brother. Barb and Jasper Owens, a couple of no-accounts that was running cattle. I didn't care one way or the other until they started messing around my friend's place. My friend wasn't much of a shooter. So I picked a fight with Jasper and gunned him down." Duke's voice was harsh. "They left my friend alone after that."

"Are you wanted by the law?"

"I wouldn't be surprised, ma'am. I had to get out of Santa Fe in a hell of a hurry."

They rode on in silence. Sarah didn't ask any more questions. She knew enough about Gibson Duke already to convince her that he was a forthright man. If he said any more, she would listen, but she would not ask any more questions.

They made camp about twenty miles outside of Dodge City late in the evening, so they could arrive in the town on to noon the next day instead of late afternoon. It was while they were drinking coffee that Duke brought the subject up again.

"I been rolling around the country since the war, ma'am," he said. "One way or another I've found myself just about to lose something or arriving too late to have a chance."

"Meaning what?"

"There was cattle in Santa Fe—I had a few head, but the fever got to them and I couldn't hold out. Then I drifted back into Texas and tried hide-hunting, but the Comanche killed my partner and took my stake. Then up north to the mining camps—" He stopped.

"Where were you raised?"

"Texas. My paw was in Houston's army when they downed old Santa Anna." He poured more coffee. "I never give much for nothing no way—that is, until—" He stopped cold.

Sarah looked him in the eye. "Until what, Mr. Duke?"

"I met you, Miss Sarah."

"That's a kind thing to say, seeing I'm a widow that's had children."

Duke began cleaning the carbine. He slipped his boots off and dug his toes into the loamy Kansas soil. "You better get some sleep, Miss Sarah. I'll just sit here a while and get this iron in shape. Dodge City is a tough place."

CHAPTER NINE

Dog City, some of the buffalo hunters called it. The summers were like the south side of hell, and the winters colder than the nose of a nuzzling buffalo calf. The small Kansas town of Dodge lay barking in the late July heat. It was a raw, ragged and mean town when Sarah and Duke rode in. Ordinarily the heat would have emptied the streets. The heat was there, and the flies and the swishing tails of the horses tied to the hitch-rails, but the streets were anything but deserted.

Twenty-five or more men milled around the general area before the Wells Fargo office, their tempers mean and their voices edged with violent protest. More than half of them carried rifles, and to the man they were armed with hand guns.

Sarah and Duke rode away from the mob, their eyes watching, trying to overhear some of the talk to learn what the trouble was.

As their ponies drifted past the milling men, a few of them turned to look at the two dirty, dust-laden riders.

"Here, let's ask them!" one of the men yelled, and pointed toward Sarah and Duke. "Hold on there, you two!" the man yelled and made a grab for Sarah's reins. Sarah pulled back and wheeled the roan up and around. The men backed off.

"Hold that horse down, damn it!" the man yelled. Others were drawn to Sarah and Duke and worked around them. Duke sat still, the carbine across his saddle. He watched Sarah pull the roan in tight.

"What's the matter with you!" the man demanded. "Ain't you got no better sense—" He made another grab for Sarah's reins and Duke leaned over, cracking the man's wrist with the barrel of the carbine. The man jerked back.

"That ain't your horse, they ain't your reins, I don't see you wearing a star, so you ain't the law. So keep your goddam hands off," Duke said in measured tones.

"Don't let him get away with that, Stu!" someone yelled to the man.

Duke looked around, threw a shell into the carbine and pulled it up. "I *got* away with it." he said, eyes alert, and hands steady.

"We got a right to know—"

"You ain't got no goddam right at all as long as I got the carbine and you ain't," Duke said. Sarah had moved to his side.

"One of 'em's a woman!" someone gasped.

"No wonder he lit into Stu!" another replied.

"Take your hat off, Miss Sarah," Duke said softly.

Sarah removed her hat and did not react to the mild ripple of amazement that ran through the group of men.

Duke looked down at the man called Stu. "If you'll tell me what this is all about and ask me politely, I might be able to help you."

"Two days ago the bank was held up by three men— but they had three more scattered through town that helped them out," Stu said. "The sheriff went after 'em with a posse, and then three hours ago about a dozen riders came into town and hit the Wells Fargo office for every ounce of dust and every eagle they had in the safe."

Duke nodded. "And you think we had something to do with it?"

"I didn't say that," Stu said. "All I wanted to do was ask you if you had seen anyone—"

"Seen lots of things."

"I tell you he's being smart and sassy—" Stu turned to yell at the others.

"He sure as hell is!" cried a cowhand gleefully. "And you're gettin' it, Stu!"

The crowd laughed and slapped their legs.

When they had quieted down, Duke nodded to the others. "As it happens, me and this lady did see riders —but this was yesterday afternoon, close on to sundown. Two groups—one seemed to be running and the other chasing after them. But we didn't see anything else."

"How do we know that's all you saw?" Stu demanded.

Duke slipped out of the saddle and stepped toward the man. "You don't know," he said. "And I'm getting tired of your big mouth. I heard Dodge City was a tough town, but I never thought it was full of windbags too."

"You call me a windbag?" Stu dropped his hand toward his side. Duke did not hesitate, he rammed the barrel of the carbine into the other man's stomach and brought his knee up into the man's face when he bent over. The blood spurted out of his nose and he dropped into the dust at Duke's feet. Duke looked at the others. "Me and this lady just came off the trail. I told you what we saw and that's all there is. We don't know anything about a bank robbery—or Wells Fargo or anything else. Only reason this had to happen was for the reasons you saw. I ain't apologizing, to him, or to any of his friends that might be in the crowd. Where I come from, we got more respect for women."

He faced the men and then deliberately put his back to them and climbed back into the saddle.

"What happened to your hand guns?" demanded an edgy voice from the crowd.

"Ran into some Comanche back a ways and lost 'em."

"That's easy to say," the voice said, and Duke saw a youngish-looking man, whip-thin and red-haired, hat pushed back to reveal a curly forelock.

Stu, with the help of several others, was pulled out of the dust and half carried through the crowd. "What you said about apologizing to Stu—or any of his friends in the crowd—I'm a friend of Stu's."

"Funny," Duke said with a grin and a glance at the others, "that you waited until he was knocked cold before you said anything. Could be that he don't know anything about it."

The young man turned red. The crowd of men began to chuckle and then laughed outright. Duke ignored the red-haired youth and nodded to Sarah. They wheeled their ponies around and moved down the street, the laughter of the crowd trailing after them.

Duke had ridden twenty-five yards when he heard the shrill demand come from behind. "You got a gun!" he heard the red-haired boy scream. "Turn around and face me!"

Duke continued to ride, the hair on the back of his neck stiffening, the muscles in his legs jerking slightly.

"I'm warning you, mister!" the voice screamed. "Turn around and git off that horse!"

"What are you going to do?" Sarah asked in a whisper, not daring to glance at him.

"Keep riding, Miss Sarah. Git up to the corner of that building there, and when I say the word, git up the alley."

"You can't fight him—"

"Do what I say, damn it!" Duke demanded. "Here it comes—now."

They were nearing the corner of the building. Sarah could see the alley leading to the rear of the structure.

"I'm going to count three, mister!" the redhead yelled.

"Go!" Duke snapped at Sarah. She jerked her reins hard and the roan leaped out of the main street into the protection of the alley.

At the instant Duke yelled for Sarah to gain cover, he slipped his saddle and fell flat and hard into the dust, the carbine up and ready. "Drop your iron, Red," he called. "I got witnesses to prove you threatened me—and I got the drop on you. Now drop your iron!"

The crowd around the young gunfighter faded into the sunbaked street and found refuge in buildings and behind wagons. Suddenly there was silence—dead, baking, fly-buzzing silence and the redhead was alone. Duke pulled down on the young man's head. "I'm giving you a count of three, Red—drop your iron and walk away or I'll kill you."

A fly landed on Duke's nose and crawled around leisurely in the sweat-grimed creases of the cow man's face. "One!"

Red did not move.

"Two!"

Red's hands began to inch for his gun.

Duke did not count three. The young man drew and Duke shot him neatly between the eyes. The bright new pearl-handled Colt had not even cleared leather. Duke got up slowly and walked toward the figure in the dust. Slowly the others began to edge out and walk toward the dead gunfighter.

Duke stared at the first of the arrivals. "I shot him in a fair fight. You all saw me try and walk away from him, and then I gave him a chance to drop his gun—"

"You don't need to do no explainin' to us, mister," said an old man. "Red here's been asking for this a long 'ime."

"He got any folks?" Duke asked.

"Not's anybody knows. He drifted into town about six months ago and just been hanging around working once in a while ever since."

Duke nodded. "That's all there is, I reckon," he said quietly.

He turned and walked back to the edge of the building where Sarah waited for him. She handed him the reins to the black without a word. Their eyes met for a moment and there was a flicker of warmth in Sarah's glance as Duke climbed into the saddle.

He turned and looked back down the middle of the street. "I think we better get ourselves a little coffee, beans and salt, and them guns, and keep moving, Miss Sarah," he said. "Everybody's got friends—some kind of friends that would hate to see you git killed."

"Doesn't it matter that it was a fair fight?" Sarah asked.

"No, ma'am. It don't matter."

Sarah nodded. "There's a hardware store down the street." She pulled out the little bag of double eagles, held back two and handed the rest to Duke. "You get two of the best guns you can, Mr. Duke, and another carbine. I'll find a store and buy the other things."

"In an hour." He nodded. "On the west side of town."

"In an hour." They rode off. The crowd of men had broken up. The body of Red had been removed.

An hour and a half later, Sarah sat beneath a cottonwood tree and waited for Duke. She stirred the coffee gently and then rolled up the legs of the new trousers she had bought for herself. To one side lay two new shirts and a thick fleece jacket, for herself, and a heavy blanket for Duke.

Duke arrived in a few minutes and they sat in silence drinking coffee and examining the brand new Colts and the fine Sharps. Sarah tested her gun and was satisfied, blushing at the admiration in Duke's face for her accuracy. Duke, when trying his own gun out, tried to outshoot her, but could do no better.

"Any reason for us to stay around here?" Sarah asked.

"I can't think of any, Miss Sarah, now that we can't find any kind of work—"

Sarah nodded. "I've been thinking, Mr. Duke, about what you said—you know, hide hunting." Sarah handled the Sharps. "We could try our hand at it—I think I would prefer that to trying my hand at something in a town."

"It's a good idea, ma'am, and we ain't got too much money left."

"I wasn't thinking so much about the money as the chances of getting One Nest during the summer, when he could be spread over hell and gone. But in the winter, when the snow comes, he'll more'n likely head for the warm places, and there ain't too many places he could go to git warm."

"You mean to store up for a winter search, ma'am?" Duke asked.

Sarah pulled the roan around. "A winter search, Mr. Duke."

Duke pulled the brim of his hat down low. "Yes, ma'am," he said. In the saddle, they leaned into the sun reluctantly and left the shade of the cottonwood clump. "Might try for bluffer northwest, Miss Sarah," Duke said. "Up toward the South and North Platte and around Frenchman Creek."

"Anything you say, Mr. Duke," Sarah said, feeling a peculiar lightheartedness. Later in the day, she thought about the redheaded young man and Duke, and the easy way he had stood up to the bully, Stu. Sarah loathed and detested violence, but she recognized courage when she saw it, and the warm admiring glance she had for Duke, which he did not see, was the look of approval a woman in doubt will finally give a man she has begun to like.

CHAPTER TEN

THEY MOVED EASILY, drifting before the winds when it was possible, wearing handkerchief masks when they had to fight the fine powdery dust blowing head-on. They made camp often, not pushing their horses, riding in the coolest parts of the day and breaking regularly for a two- to three-hour midday rest, sleeping in the shade of their ponies when they could not find cover.

They were nine days out of Dodge City when they began to pick up their first buffalo, a small stand that was working into the grass well upwind of them. Duke cautioned Sarah to remain quiet while he rode down close to them and looked them over. He slipped his saddle a thousand yards down from the contented animals, broke out the brand-new Sharps, sighted down on a young calf and fired.

From her position Sarah saw the animal drop as if felled by an ax. The herd did not even look up. One of the old bulls was only a few feet away and was curious enough to walk over and smell the dead calf, but none of the others bothered.

Sarah watched, and unconsciously nodded her appreciation for the manner in which Duke had made his move against the small stand without disturbing them. She was about to move out into the open when she heard the unmistakable click of a cocked gun.

"Just don't move or make a motion to your partner. And sit still!"

The voice was old, but hard. Sarah remained motionless, watching Duke return from his position in the grass, glancing back over his shoulder to look at the stand and then looking around the flat country. He made his black and turned at a trot back to Sarah.

Sarah's eyes traveled to the gun. He had slipped the rifle back into the boot and he was riding straight in the saddle, not aware of danger, and not in position to draw his Colt. She stared at him, frowning, straining every muscle in her face to warn him of the danger, but the cowman grinned in return, thinking about the sun and the way it made her frown.

"At least we'll eat tender beef tonight, Miss Sarah—" Duke began.

The voice in back of Sarah cut him off. "Step down, gents, or I'll take both of you at once with a load of buckshot."

Duke jerked up straight in the saddle and looked beyond Sarah into the shadows of the cottonwood. He squinted his eyes.

There was movement behind Sarah and the owner of the voice stepped out. "I said step down, gents!"

He was an old man, sweat-grimed and filthy, in buckskin whose fringe was long since gone. He wore a Colt .45 in a beaded holster and a sweat-stained, weather-beaten old hat. His beard was a full foot long and came to a curious point on his chest. The beard was jet-black, and what little hair Duke and Sarah could see at the edges of his hat was snow-white. He smiled, but there was no friendliness in his eyes, the coldest and blackest Sarah had ever seen. The shotgun leveled on them was old and steady.

"Drop your irons in the dust and easy does it, gents," he said with a slight nod of his head.

Sarah and Duke unbuckled the new belts and dropped their guns to the ground. "Now step away from them, easy-like."

They moved away.

"If you're going to shoot, do it." Duke said. "But this is a woman—"

"Woman!" he looked closely at Sarah. "Damned if it ain't!"

"That don't excuse you pulling down on us." Duke said.

"What'cha doing out here in the middle of nowheres?"

"None of your business." Duke replied testily. "You better shoot—"

"Aw, hell, mister," the old man said, lowering the gun, "I don't go around shooting people. Leastwise women." He stepped forward and offered his hand to Duke. "My name's Slater—"

Duke moved to accept the old man's hand and then quickly knocked him down and grabbed for the shotgun.

The old man shook his head and felt his jaw. "Damn, you hit hard," he said, and started to get up.

"Sit still," Duke said, and Sarah looked at him quickly. But she sighed silently to herself, seeing that Duke's anger was fading fast at the sudden switch in the old man's attitude. "How come you to have thrown down on us like that?" Duke demanded. "We didn't do nothing to you."

The old man frowned. "You damned fool." he said, and then glanced at Sarah. "I beg your pardon ma'am; didn't mean to cuss."

"Get up," Duke said wearily.

"I been scouting this stand of bluffer for four days."

"They belong to the man that gets them," Duke said. He lowered the gun and extended his hand to the old man and helped him to his feet. "All I did was shoot a little eating meat."

"Ain't the meat I begrudge you, son," the old man said, still feeling his jaw; "It's the Indians your shot will bring down."

Duke shook his head and handed the gun over. "I sure made a mess of things, didn't I?"

"You damn sure might of. I coulda been skinning out by now instead of sitting around on my hind end these last four days if it weren't for the Cheyenne," the old man complained. "Been sitting over that ridge yonder waiting for 'em to get out of the country so I could get about my work, but they got some kind of medicine they're tending to on the flats down toward the Republican River and ain't nothing going to move them until they're ready."

"You think they heard the shot?"

The old man made a face of disgust. "After blasting away with that thing of yourn, and the Injun partly downwind, what do you think." He shook his head. "My goodness, it's been a long time since I seen a woman that looked purty in man's pants."

"Careful," Duke said.

"I'm careful," the old man said. "Touchy, ain't he?" he said to Sarah.

"And you, Mr. Slater?" Sarah said with a soft smile.

"You're right, ma'am, I guess we all are." He turned suddenly and moved with amazing speed and grace for an old man, and right before their eyes disappeared into the brush. He reappeared a moment later and made a gesture toward the river. "They're coming, all right, mister."

Duke had slipped into his saddle and now stood above Slater. "If Cheyennes are coming, we're leaving," he said. "You coming along?"

"Soon as I can get that calf beef you dropped."

"Where's your horse?"

"I got three—two pack animals—over the side of the trees. Didn't you see me when you came over the rise?" Duke shook his head. "Disgusting, that's what it is. I coulda had you clean shot before you knew what hit you if I was mean."

"Go get your horses. I'll get the calf." Duke said.

"Watching you sneak up on that stand, you must have done a bit of bluffer skinning yourself at one time or other," Slater said casually, not making any move away from them.

"Listen, are there Indians coming or not?" Duke demanded nervously.

"I said they was, didn't I?"

"Then let's get moving."

Slater looked up at Sarah and grinned. "Ve-ry touchy —ve-ry touchy." He dropped back into the brush and trees and disappeared again with the same speed and grace.

"I'll have to spook that herd," Duke said. "You better stay with me, Miss Sarah."

They rode out into the sun again, driving straight for the stand of buffalo. They got no closer than two thousand yards when the animals bolted, jerking around in a circle after a maddened old bull, and then broke away to the north directly for the Indians.

There was no time to do a proper job of butchering the calf, but by the time Slater pulled up, Duke had taken the hindquarters and forked them over one of the pack horses of the old hunter.

Duke rode to the crest of the ridge that looked out over the grass flats and saw the trail of dust the stampeding herd of buffalo had lifted. He watched for a long time and then saw the party of six full-dressed Cheyenne sprinting toward the ridge and the thick bunch of cottonwood trees. Duke spurred the black and rode back to Sarah and the old man. "They're coming hard, and we'd better get out or fight."

"How many?" Slater asked.

"Six."

The old man nodded. "We better run. If they was just curious they woulda just sent out two or three. But whatever they're powwowing about over to the river, they don't want nobody to know about it. This party of six means business—and if they don't come back, then there'll be six times six to come lookin' for 'em, I reckon." He handed one of the lead ropes of the pack horses to Duke. "We'd be better off if we struck south and to the west, gettin' away from the river area and what's going on."

"Let's go, then."

The old man rode a fine sorrel that had energy and speed. They broke away from the ridge and turned due south, their dust kicking up high and leaving a trail the Cheyenne could follow if they wanted to. But neither Duke nor Slater felt the Indians would follow.

They rode hard for several hours, leaving the sandy ridge and grass country and hitting the hard flatlands beyond the edges of Beaver River tributaries and slowed to a walk, breathing their horses.

It was dark when the old man, who had ridden ahead of them, pulled into a small box canyon created by two small buttes and a sagebrush thicket at one end. "They won't come after us now, so we might as well take this place for the night," he commented. Without another word, he began making preparations for a fire.

Sarah was tired, but she began to inspect the hindquarters of the buffalo calf, skinning it out more carefully and preparing it for cooking. Duke took care of the horses, staking them out in grass and near water and bringing all their saddles and gear close into the fire.

The night closed in heavy and black and the night noises took over the silences that lay between the three riders. Off some distance a coyote yelled and moved on. There was the rustle of a small animal in the thicket of sage. The stars dropped out of the black velvet overhead. Sarah put on coffee water and the three sat down to stare into the flames and think their own thoughts, Sarah occasionally prodding a thick cut of the beef hung over the low, hot coal fire the old hunter had made.

They ate in silence, and Duke was the only one to speak as he wiped his hands on his shirt and reached for the carbine. "I'll take the first watch," he said and moved off to the head of the canyon.

After a moment, Slater raised his head. "Been married long?"

"He's not my husband," Sarah said.

"I beg your pardon, ma'am," Slater said, respect and apology in his voice. "Good night." He rolled over where he sat and was asleep in thirty seconds.

CHAPTER ELEVEN

THE CHEYENNE party of six did not follow them. But Sarah, Duke and Slater remained in the protected position of the small canyon for the next two days, taking turns on guard, eating and sleeping. When the last of the calf buffalo was gone and there was still no sign of the Indians, Duke and Slater seemed satisfied they were in the clear.

"Well," Slater said, "looks like we can move on our ways. Though I sure hated to see that stand of bluffer stampede away from me. Been hunting meat all spring and never hit more than twenty or thirty." He shook his head. "Sure beats me how a man's luck can run sometimes."

"We're sorry about messing up your hunt party, Slater," Duke said.

There had been very little talk among the three during their wait for the Cheyenne to show up. After Slater's one question to Sarah about marriage, he had clammed up and not opened his mouth in a personal way to either of them again. And when Sarah and Duke offered no explanations, nor questioned him, their remarks were confined to chores and the simple scouting sorties made from the canyon to search out a noise or an animal cry that did not sound exactly right.

Slater had begun to load his pack animals. "Look here," he said suddenly. "Where you two aim to go from here?"

Duke was slow in answering. "We thought we'd try a little hide-hunting."

Slater turned and examined Duke a long time. "I don't see no gear for hide hunting."

"I got guns and skinning knives."

"I see." Slater nodded and turned back to his packing.

Duke began saddling the roan and the black. The small party was packed and ready to leave before anyone spoke again. Slater stood with the reins of his sorrel in his hand and looked at Duke and Sarah. "Now listen, I'm an old stinkweed that ain't got no particular reason for saying what I'm about to say, but I'm going to say it."

"I promise I won't take offense," Duke said soberly.

"All right. Now here's the way I see it. I got all the trimmings for a solid summer of hide-hunting—" he waved his hand at the two pack animals—" but I'm getting old and lazy. Time was when I thought I'd make me a big stake on killing bluffer and selling hides and then light out for Texas somewheres and start me a little cattle place."

Sarah took a deep breath. The memory of her own little place and of her son and daughter and the work her husband Adam had put into the raising of the breed herd, made her turn away.

"You got an offer, Mr. Slater?" Duke asked.

"I have." Slater said. "One man can care for himself all right enough, especially this one talkin' to you. But like I said, I'm getting tired and lazy. If this lady would keep camp for us, cook and stuff, while you and me go out and do the killing and skinnin', why I reckon we'd do right well by ourselves before the snows come."

Duke thought about this and turned to look at Sarah. She made no sign that she had anything to say. It was plain to Duke that it was his decision to make. "What you say is fine, Mr. Slater, but didn't you just tell us that you trailed all spring and only found one little stand of meat?"

"Sure," Slater said, "that's because I been working south of the two Plattes. That Cheyenne business we run into is the reason I'm here now. One man can't go into country where the buffalo are and kill and skin and hide and cook for himself—and still keep one eye out for the Injun parties."

"Are you sure the buffalo are around the two Plattes?"

Slater nodded his head emphatically. "Scouted them myself."

Duke thought about this for a moment. "How would you want to split the earnings?"

"Well, I got a mite invested in the gear—that counts some—so I reckon if the lady will take care of the camp that's worth a full share. Let's say that we do it three ways, even, after I take out for the trappings."

Duke turned to Sarah. "It's a good proposition, Miss Sarah. If you don't have any feelings about going back into the Cheyenne country—after what happened, I mean."

Sarah nodded her head. "I think that Mr. Slater's offer is generous and I think we oughtta take it, Mr. Duke."

"Fine," Slater said and offered his hand to her, then to Duke. After they had shaken hands, he turned to look around at the sky. "Best thing for us to do is sneak into that country, and the best way to do that is ride west and come back around into Colorado and cross the South Platte at the headwaters of Frenchman Creek. I got an idea that every danged bluffer in the whole world is up there belly-deep on some of that heavy grass."

They rode out of the canyon, swung directly west and made steady time until sunset, and by the time darkness caught them they were bedded down for the night near a small stream that was jumping with fish. In half an hour Duke and Sarah had pulled a dozen out of the water, gutted them and strung them through the gills over a hot greasewood fire.

With coffee and sourdough biscuits the three partners settled down to a feast of rare delicacy. Sarah, it was established, would always take the first guard after eating and be allowed to sleep a full night without being disturbed. Duke would take the middle watch and then the old man. Duke promptly crawled off from the fire into his blanket and left Sarah and Slater alone. Sarah was just finishing her coffee before taking up a position when Slater glanced over at Duke. He listened a moment for the deep regular breathing of the thick-chested cowman and then turned back to Sarah, speaking in a low voice. "It ain't none of my business, ma'am," he said, "but I'm sure high on curiosity about how you and this fellow happen to be out here in the middle of the Indian country all by your lonesome and —beggin' your pardon ma'am—not married."

Sarah smiled. "It's not hard to explain, Mr. Slater," she said gently, with a look at the figure of Gibson Duke. Softly, and without emotion, she told the old trapper about her husband and One Nest. "At first, I thought I'd never be able to draw another breath until I had found him and killed that Injun—Let alone look at another man, to have feelings for him."

"Yes ma'am." Slater said.

"Now—" She paused. "Now, Mr. Slater, I think I might even be able to forget about One Nest. I think I understand a lot of things that pain and hate and revenge wouldn't allow me to consider when I started out. Gibson Duke helped me that way. I never met a more patient man."

"Yes ma'am." Slater said. "You don't have to say nothin' else. I understand. I'm old an' mean an' stink to high heaven because I hate taking baths—" he shook his head in annoyance—"but I sure like to see things real and honest once in a while."

Sarah picked up the Sharps and walked away toward a small crust of hill that stood about thirty feet above their position. She settled down and held the gun across her lap and stared into the darkness, looking up at the stars, letting her mind wander back over the weeks to the beginning. It all seemed like a dream. But she turned and looked at the bed of coals in the dying fire and felt the reassurance of its being real. In a moment the snores of Slater drifted up to her.

She stood up, alert, gun ready, eyes sharp and clear in the darkness, and waited for something to happen. Nothing did happen and Duke came to take her place before midnight, grumpy, sleepy and not fully awake. He grunted something to her that Sarah took for "Good night," and she went down to the blankets. She lay a moment on the hard ground and watched the vague outlines of his kneeling figure in the darkness.

CHAPTER TWELVE

SARAH AWOKE to the slight pressure on her shoulder. She opened her eyes. It was still dark. But she knew it was Duke kneeling beside her. "What is it?" she breathed silently.

"Get up quietly. We have company."

She moved out of the blankets, pulling the Colt as she stood up and looked around the camp. Slater was gone, and the fire was out. She could see the piles of dirt that had been kicked on the coals, vaguely, and the little smoke coming out of the edges.

Duke took her hand and guided her to the outer edge of the dirt ridge that had been used as a sentry post. They crawled to the edge of the top and bumped into Slater. "Where are they?" Duke asked the old man.

"Just coming into the open over yonder. Watch just below the polestar and you'll see one of them move in a minute."

"Indians?" Sarah asked in a soft whisper.

"No," Duke said. "Camp raiders."

Sarah felt Slater touch her on the back and motion for her to move further over to the right, stringing the three of them out at ten-foot intervals along the ridge.

Sarah slipped the Colt back into her holster, and laid the carbine over the crust of earth, and waited. She saw something move in the graying light. She glanced toward the east and saw the first signs of day coming up, just a smattering of gray that was nearly black. But she knew it would start coming up lighter, fast and sure. She wondered fleetingly if Duke or Slater had given any thought to trying to escape. She didn't remember their position too well, but she did know that it wasn't much of a place to make a fighting stand.

There was movement again, directly in front of her and about two hundred yards out. Just a slight, abrupt gesture that would not have been seen in the dark a few minutes before.

"See anything?" Duke asked on her right.

"Yes," she replied.

"You, Slater?"

"Yup," the old man grunted.

"I think I have one of them spotted. Want to fight, or run?"

"Fight," Slater said, spitting it out.

"All right by me," Duke said. "How about you, Miss Sarah?"

"If it's necessary," Sarah said. "But if there's any other way, I'd rather do it."

"There ain't no other way," Slater said. "These vermin are worse than Apache."

"Pick out one of them and when I give the word, fire," Duke said.

Sarah turned her attention back to the place where she had seen the movement a few minutes before. She saw it again—the barest suggestion of gleaming metal. She leveled the carbine and waited. In the silence she heard the heavy hammer of Slater's buffalo gun pulled back. Then she heard the rustle of Duke as he laid the Sharps on the ground and sighted down. "Ready?" he said quietly.

"Yup."

"Ready."

"Fire," Duke breathed.

The three guns spoke together, three sheets of flame in the darkness.

"Down!" Duke commanded. There was a scream out in front of them, then a crashing around in the darkness. A man began to gag. Then a hail of lead began to dig into the ridge they were hiding behind.

"Try and spot one of them," Duke said.

"I got two," Slater replied.

"I have one," Sarah said.

"Steady now," Duke said. "Move further apart about another ten feet and wait for the command to fire."

Sarah inched her way further away from the others and stopped at what she judged to be ten feet. She leveled the carbine again and caught sight of movement in the rapidly lightening area in front of the ridge. There was a shallow depression of thick grass that dropped off sharply into a gulch made long ago from an overwash of rain. A man's head, hatless and gray-white in the expanding morning light, popped up and then dropped down again. She sighted along the depression's edge and waited for the man's head to reappear. It did and she marked the spot.

"Ready?" Duke whispered to her.

"Yes."

She did not hear Slater's reply.

"Fire," Duke said.

Slater fired and a man screamed. She waited for her man's head to reappear again, finger on the trigger, palm flat on the barrel of the carbine, pressing it down into the dirt to keep it from dancing when she pulled the trigger. There was a long minute of silence. Then Duke fired again. And as soon as he fired, the head in Sarah's sights danced up and snapped a handgun which had been shot in Duke's direction. Sarah fired and saw the man flip backwards.

She withdrew and sat protected behind the ridge. The sky was lighting up rapidly now. She could make out the figures of Slater and Duke plainly. She looked down at Duke and nodded that she was all right. Slater moved back toward the middle section of the ridge and spoke quietly to Duke. They both turned and looked up toward the camp where the horses were staked. The fire from the other side of the ridge began to grow steadily stronger. Sarah listened to the different sound the guns made. She counted five different guns, listening to the reports and checking the pattern of the man firing. Duke and Slater were nodding. Slater slipped down the edge of the ridge and into their camp and made his way toward the horses. He saddled his sorrel quickly and leaped into leather. He nodded to Duke, who then worked his way down to where Sarah had resumed her position on the edge of the ridge.

"Slater is going to try and get around them and make for that hillock back yonder." He nodded toward the opposite side of the depression. "That way we can get them in a crossfire. Use your Colt and get ready to cover him when he makes a run for it."

Sarah drew the Colt, examined it, and nodded that she was ready. Duke had his gun out, and moved back to his position. He nodded to Slater, who drew his handgun and spurred the sorrel in the flanks. The animal leaped ahead with amazing energy and speed and the old hunter, leaning low on the off-side, firing over his saddlehorn, broke free of the ridge cover and headed straight out for the plains and grass country.

Immediately Sarah and Duke emptied their Colts into the line opposite them and did not attempt accuracy in their shooting, just a covering fire. A few of the answering guns in the depression broke away from the head-on fight and began firing at Slater, but the breakneck speed of the sorrel was too much, plus the element of surprise, and Slater was out of range and circling hard and fast in back of the raiders hardly before they knew what was going on.

Duke and Sarah reloaded one at a time and sat back to wait.

Suddenly Sarah heard a crunching noise to her side. She whirled and fired. She caught the man in the right leg. He stumbled and nearly fell, but steadied himself and brought up his gun again.

Sarah fired quickly and shot him in the heart. She dropped in a heap and lay still. Duke watched from his position, and Sarah could see his face go white from twenty feet away.

There was a distant booming now, a loud, heavy report that was much deeper and more solid than any of the sharper noises of the carbines and Colts used on both sides.

Duke indicated the other side of the raiders. Sarah sneaked a look, sticking her head above the ridge, and had her hat shot off. She dropped back down.

The heavy report came again. Duke grinned. "Slater's gun—a big Ballard fifty—he's so far out of range they can't hope to get back at him. They either have to run or stay here and get it."

It didn't take the raiders long to decide. In a few minutes and after several more of the booming shots from Slater's buffalo gun, Sarah and Duke heard the sudden rush of hoofs beating a retreat back to the south. Carbine up and ready, Sarah winged a couple of shots after them but the five remaining men escaped to the nearly yellow sky of the morning.

Slowly, Duke leading the way, they inched out from behind the cover of the ridge and stepped over to the depression. Seven men lay on the ground. One of them was still alive, but only barely so. He tried to speak.

Sarah leaned over quickly and picked the man's head up and rested it in her lap. The man tried to smile—and then closed his eyes.

Slater came in a few minutes later. He looked around at the dead bodies and danced a jig. "Damnation! Once I got this old hump killer hot and working, they sure lit out like an Injun chile after his first drink of fire water!"

Sarah stood up. "Who are they?" Her face was drained of color.

Duke took her by the shoulder. "Raiders. Saddlebums of one kind and another. Don't feel bad about it, Miss Sarah. It was them or us. And I don't have to tell you what they would have done if they had gotten you alive."

"Yes." Instinctively, Sarah trembled as she saw the grinning and excited Slater going through the pockets of the dead men.

"God! What a fight! Damn it, Miss Sarah, you're better with a shooter than any four men I ever saw." Slater held up a gold watch and listened for the tick. "Works, too!" He shoved it into his pocket.

All the rest of the day Duke and Slater worked, digging out shallow graves to bury the dead. They selected two of the best rifles, took all the shells, and Duke rode out to round up the horses. . . .

That night as they sipped coffee and Duke and Slater talked over the fight again and again, Sarah remained silent, wondering about the land that was so full of death and hardship. She wondered if it would not have been better to remain in Georgia after the war—even all the hardships to endure there—rather than this.

Without a word she took her carbine and walked back to the ridge position on her first guard of the night, and looked down at the shallow graves of the seven men she had helped to kill. Nameless, meaningless, death. She thought a long time about the revenge killing of One Nest.

CHAPTER THIRTEEN

THEY MOVED into the headwaters of the Republican a week later and crossed the river well into Colorado and then turned north, traveling at a steady daylight-to-dusk pace without a break, stopping only at noon to make coffee and pull at smoked meat cooked the night before.

It was toward the middle of August and the heat was parching and the land was dry when they moved into the watershed area of the South Platte and trailed northeast along the river's edge and crossed back into Nebraska. On the seventeenth of August they topped a butte and stood staring out over the deep valley that Slater called Hansen's Place. Below them, hemmed in on three sides of the valley, were more buffalo than Sarah had ever seen.

"There they are," Slater said, pulling his kerchief down off his face to hang on his beard. "Meat on the table and skins for the asking. We make camp right here, Miss Sarah."

Duke slipped his saddle and pulled out an ax from one of the packs on the trailing horses. He began working on a group of poplars for hide racks and a makeshift corral. Slater dropped down the gentle slope leading into the valley and began scouting the herd, working his way around slowly, watching for signs of Indians and studying the hills. Sarah set about establishing a fireplace with stones, building the campsite near a stream and clearing the grass away from the cooking area. Dry as tinder, the slightest spark would have set the brush to burning. That night they went to sleep early and arose before dawn, and by the second night, Duke and Slater had built half a dozen hide racks and a good-sized corral for the horses.

In the morning Sarah was left alone as the two men took their guns and knives and two pack horses each and dropped down ino the valley. About an hour after sun-up, Sarah began to hear the rolling boom of their rifles echoing and re-echoing. At noon, the shooting stopped and Sarah knew they were turning now to the skinning.

Having prepared a simple meal for the two men, she climbed the roan and made her way into the valley. Duke had killed more than thirty buffalo and was busy skinning them down, trimming the skin away from the hoofs, slitting up the belly to the throat, around the throat and then down the inside of each leg to the belly cut. A rope was made fast to a section of the skin and looped to the saddle of his black, which kept an even, though slight, strain on the rope. As Duke peeled the thick hide from the tissue and flesh, the horse pulled the animal's hide from its body.

Duke was bloody from head to boot. Sarah left his food and rode out into the valley several miles to find Slater in the same condition, only having killed nearly twice as many animals as Duke had.

That night they came into camp well after dark, their pack horses weighted down with skins. They didn't stop to eat before they had put the skins in the racks, watered and fed the horses and washed some of the buffalo blood from their bodies.

Slater ate with relish and was asleep the minute the meal was finished. Duke could not eat his full meal, leaning backwards with his plate in his hand, and he slept without moving until dawn the next morning.

From the middle of August until the middle of September, when the first cold winds began to come out of the northwest, they shot and skinned and shot and skinned and shot and skinned.

Sarah would spend her days hunting out berries and nuts and shooting small game to keep a variety in the meals, riding down into the valley with their noon meal and back again to the campsite.

At the first sign of cold weather, Sarah began building a sod hut, cutting the poplar trees herself and digging the corner posts for the frames, lashing the beams and light tree trunks together with green buffalo hide that dried to steel-hard fastness.

The first of November they counted up their hides as the buffalo began to leave the valley and drift toward the south.

"I count close on to eighteen hundred," Slater said.

"That ought to be enough to keep us fair for a while. Now we got to start 'em into Cheyenne." He glanced up at the skies. "We can pack some on the animals, but we're going to have to get us some wagons for the rest of them."

Duke agreed that it would be best to pack as many on the horses as possible, get money to buy wagons and come back for the rest. But there was the element of beating the weather. In six weeks the country would be frozen solid.

For three days they worked, packing camp, getting ready to leave, and finally loading the horses. On the fifth of November there was a light snow as they moved away from the valley and headed due west along the banks of the South Platte, toward Cheyenne.

Sarah's hair had grown back quite a bit and was clear over her neck, and her strong face had been burned deep brown by the sun. The clothes she bought in Dodge City had long since worn out and she had taken a buffalo calf skin and worked it and beaten it into softness, leaving an edging of fur at the collar of her jacket. Duke had also discarded his Dodge City clothes and wore leather now.

Three days later they hit Lodgepole Creek and kept pushing west, fighting the cold one day, and burning up in the hot November sun the next. They covered the last hundred miles of their trek in three days, and pulled into Cheyenne.

Duke and Slater sold the hides and bought wagons and pulled out the next day, leaving Sarah alone.

The first hard snow came on Thanksgiving Day and she sat alone in the hotel room wearing a dress for the first time since she had left Texas. She stared out the window at the tracks the solitary riders up and down the Cheyenne streets made as they moved from one saloon to another.

On December fifteenth, Slater and Duke returned with the remaining hides and they divided more than six thousand dollars after selling the extra horses and wagons.

They celebrated with a big dinner, and Slater announced that he was going to remain in Cheyenne. "Miss Sarah, I have no bones about telling you and Duke here how I feel about you two. I wish you'd give up this idea of getting that Indian, and pool our stake into cattle and a place around here. You two could get married—"

"Thank you, Mr. Slater," Sarah said firmly, "but there is something you don't understand—"

It didn't take Duke long to add his own voice. He and Slater had seen fine lands in their movement through the country, and with the railroad in Cheyenne, there was a good chance of their succeeding.

Sarah listened to both of them quietly and patiently. Then she turned to Duke. "Mr. Duke, I hesitate to remind you that until now I have not asked for your help or assistance. I intend leaving Cheyenne in the morning, heading south. Alone, if that proves necessary."

Slater shook his head. "Well, Miss Sarah, after being with you all these weeks and months. I know you for a strong-minded, fearless woman, with her own reasons for everything. I ain't going to say no more."

"We might be back—" Duke said tentatively.

"Yes, Mr. Slater, we might be back."

"I ain't promising I'll be here," Slater said. He looked around the restaurant. "Might just head for California and see if some of that sunshine won't help me a bit."

"Mr. Duke, I have to get an early start in the morning."

Duke nodded. They stood up. Slater shook hands with both of them, not trying to hide the tears in his eyes. "Damn it, I wished I was twenty years younger." He glared at Duke. "I'd beat your head in to stand beside this woman like you're doing." He grabbed Sarah roughly and kissed her, then turned and stalked out of the room.

Duke took a deep breath and turned away. Sarah walked out of the restaurant and back to her hotel. She got down on her knees. She began to pray, asking if she was doing a Christian thing to press her search for One Nest.

She came to no decision. She looked out the window and saw Gibson Duke walking slowly toward a saloon. He stood there before the glass door looking inside, as if undecided, then pushed the doors open and entered. Just before the door closed, Sarah saw a painted and flashy blonde in a red dress take his arm.

CHAPTER FOURTEEN

THEY NEVER SAW Slater again. They left the next morning with the day bright and hard and clear. Sarah had bought new trousers and shirts and boots and wore the fleece-lined jacket bought in Dodge City. The horses snorted with energy in the crisp morning, their hoofs crunching through the crusted snow, and breaking the silence of the frozen Wyoming country.

Duke was silent. His eyes were red and his hands trembled. Sarah had seen enough men drinking in her lifetime to know that Duke was not feeling quite right. She did not mind the drinking, but when she thought about the blonde, painted girl, she clenched her teeth.

They knew each other well enough and had been on the trail long enough now to do their camp chores and ride trail for days without speaking.

They worked their way down from South Platte and then headed to the east to escape the Ute they had heard were making trouble. The cold became intense and they had a daily grind of fighting to keep warm. The fires at night were hard to get going and there was little for the horses to eat.

They camped for several days along the mouth of the Republican River, holed up in a small cave they had luckily found, while a blizzard blew itself out. Neither of them had mentioned Slater or the last night in Cheyenne since leaving, but the enforced confinement in the cave brought things to a head.

"You got something on your mind, Miss Sarah?" Duke said finally.

"I sure have, Mr. Duke." she replied.

"All right, out with it."

"I have it on my mind and not on my tongue, sir," she said curtly.

"That's a hell of a way to behave," he said. "Damn it, this has gotten to be the craziest situation anyone ever heard of."

Sarah remained silent.

"I suppose you thinking about that last night in Cheyenne?"

"I have no obligation to you, Mr. Duke," she replied, "and you are mistaken if you think you have one toward me."

"If you call loving somebody an obligation, then I got one."

"Me?" Sarah asked and Duke looked up, surprised at the strange manner and the surprising annoyance he heard in her voice.

"Who the hell else?" Duke demanded.

"I thought it might be—" Sarah paused—"a yellow-haired girl with paint on her face."

Duke's mouth fell open. He stared at her. "Well, I'll be God-damned!"

He got up and stomped out of the cave and into the snow and did not return until it was dark. He came in and sat down beside the fire and nodded his head toward the mouth of their cave. "It's still pretty cold."

Sarah turned to him. "Mr. Duke," she said, her voice steady, "I guess it's time we had an understanding."

"Yes ma'am," Duke said.

"I won't sleep with you until I've married you. And I won't marry you until I've come to some conclusion about this Injun."

Sarah's bluntness shocked the cowman into wide-eyed amazement.

"Furthermore," she continued, "I want you to know that I have no right whatsoever to question your behavior, or your actions, or your friends. And I apologize for—" she stopped.

She grabbed her coffee cup and took a long drink and stared into the fire.

"Yes ma'am," Duke said. He grinned. He rolled back into the blanket and looked at her. "I told that black horse of mine that you was something, Miss Sarah, and damned if you ain't." He grinned at her again and rolled over, putting his back to the fire, and went to sleep.

Sarah got up and began brushing the roan furiously. The pony stamped around and pulled away. "Stand still, damnit!" Sarah said with exasperation.

Duke began to snore. "Shut up!" Sarah yelled and threw the thick bunch of pine needles at Duke's head.

He jerked up, and looked at her. "Ma'am?"

"Oh, go to sleep!"

"Yes ma'am," he said, and rolled over to his blanket again.

"*Ohhhh!*" Sarah's fury made her stalk out of the cave into the darkness.

It took them two weeks to get down into the Texas Panhandle, and in the whole time they did not see another living thing. It seemed that the thick carpet of snow had swooped down out of the north and washed everything but themselves before it, and covered what would not move. When they came to the end of the snow as they continued their move to the south, the hard, biting winds that swept across the flats bit into them relentlessly. Sarah's hands chapped so badly they cracked open and began to bleed. Duke had torn a hole in his hat and now wore a strip of his blanket around his head and under his chin to cover his ears. They rode very little, not moving on until the sun came up—if it came up at all—and bedding down early in the afternoon if they found good cover for themselves and the animals. Their food consisted of any meat they could shoot. Their coffee ran out and once they rode three days without hitting water and then it took Duke three hours to chop through the thick ice covering the stream, to find that the creek had frozen solid and finally ended up melting down ice in the coffee pot.

Several times they had to sleep snuggled up to their horses, out in the raw open when they passed over a big dry that offered not so much cover as a blade of grass or a thick brush.

It was January when they began to drift toward the southwest, moving into the great open plains of west Texas. There they saw their first Indian.

They moved on, hardly able to keep their eyes into the biting wind to watch the movements of the man, seeing that it was an Apache. The further south they got, the less the sun hid behind gray skies and slowly, little by little, they began to see the character of the land change before them. It wasn't green, but there were things growing, and even this little bit of life seemed to give them renewed hope.

They continued on south and west across the Plains

seeing cattle grazing now and then, moving away from the solitary riders, catching sight of a deer now and then, scrawny and hungry, but with the exception of the single Apache, they saw no Indians, or signs of them.

They were nearly to the Pecos when they broke camp one morning and heard the distant thunder of hooves pounding the frozen ground. They mounted quickly and worked their way deeper into the chaparral they had stopped in and waited.

To the east and out of the sun, across one of the sandy frozen outcropping hills of southern bluffs along the New Mexico line, they saw at least fifty Comanche braves in paint and feathers. They were riding hard.

"It's some kind of a fight," Duke said. "With who and where is anybody's guess."

"What's closer than Little Ben?"

Duke nodded, his lips were pressed tightly together. "That's it," he said. "This is a hard winter. They're probably going after cattle around Little Ben."

"I wonder," Sarah said, watching the Indians move across their path, "if that heathen One Nest is in that bunch."

"There ain't but one way to find out, Miss Sarah."

"Let's go."

"If we cut straight across the flats to the south, we might be able to outrun them into town. But they'll see us."

"Well, there ain't much else we can do, is there, Mr. Duke?"

"No, ma'am, I don't guess there is."

Both the black and the roan were tired and thinned down after the long hard trailing down from the Wyoming country, but both animals put on their best speed. Duke and Sarah stayed with the cover of the chaparral as long as they could, but after a few minutes they broke clear of it and were exposed to the Indians on their flank. Duke kept a lookout for them to swerve away from their line of direction and head for them. He and Sarah needed only a few minutes' break on their course to be ahead of the Indians. They broke over a rise just as the Indians were topping another some distance away. Over his shoulder Duke saw the line of their ride falter slightly and then turn in their direction. But he breathed easier. If the black and the roan would stand it, they could beat the onrushing party by a mile into the town of Little Ben.

They slaked out now, Sarah and Duke a good two miles ahead of the Indian party, riding low and forward in the saddle, the bright sun beating down on them, cold wind whipping in their faces.

Sarah glanced over her shoulder. The party seemed to be gaining. Duke saw it too, and pointed to their left, toward a low, crusty butte with a sheer wall of red frozen earth a quarter of a mile ahead and several miles long. They changed their line of ride slightly and made for the butte.

The two horses were nearly winded now. The black was stronger than the roan and began to pull ahead. Duke slowed his horse slightly to stay at Sarah's side. Then they were at the wall of the butte and the animals were digging into the hard sides with their forelegs, kicking hard with their back quarters slipping and sliding, but gaining height. The Indians were gaining on them now, and Sarah could hear their shouts and the drumming of their ponies' hooves on the frozen ground.

They made the top of the butte at last and just as Duke had figured, the ground leveled off for several miles straight ahead of them.

Something moved in the distance. It was too big to be a horse and rider, yet it had moved. Sarah and Duke saw it at the same time, wondering, and then as they drew nearer they saw that it was cattle.

They drew nearer and saw the chuckwagon then, and began to make out figures on horseback. Duke drew his Colt and fired into the air, rapidly, watching the riders and the cattle.

The riders ahead of them stopped and looked, then began to lope out to meet them. Duke glanced around. The Indians had not been heading for Little Ben—they were going to make a raid on the cattle. And the height of the butte would keep them hidden until they were right on top of the cattle.

Duke and Sarah flew past the outriders. "Indians!" Duke yelled and swept past the cowboys, who wheeled their ponies around and began to ride after them.

Duke made straight for the chuckwagon and the collection of buffalo-hide tents. Men began to appear out of their shelters and from in back of the wagon. The cattle parted before them, bellowing and stumbling awkwardly in the cold.

Sarah and Duke slammed to a stop before the wagon. A tall man in a red undershirt ran toward them. "What the hell's going on!"

"Indians, mister! Down off the butte. They're going to come up over that wall any minute if you don't get over there and keep 'em off!" Duke pointed to the drop that would lead to the lower plains.

Half a dozen men came running up buckling on guns and pulling on fleece jackets. There was a lot of noise from the cattle and the men began to shout among themselves. The big man in the red undershirt bellowed in a voice louder than Duke had ever heard on a human being before. "Never mind the horses, get to that wall yonder!" he roared.

The men turned and ran across the frozen ground in their Texas boots, jackets and coats flapping in the cold wind, loading their guns, pulling at ammunition belts and pulling their hats down against the bite of the cold.

Sarah and Duke wheeled their horses around and pounded up to the edge of the drop and were followed by the outriders they had met coming in. A quarter of a mile away the Indian party had spread out into a point and were driving to get up the wall.

Sarah and Duke dismounted and slapped their animals away from the line of fire. The others in the cattle camp came running up then and began taking up positions along the rim of the butte.

For a thousand yards the cowboys spread out and steeled themselves against the cold and watched the Comanches driving in.

"Hold your fire until I give the word!" the big man in the red shirt bellowed. He was pulling at his hat and at a fleece coat and trying to buckle on a gunbelt all at once. "Give 'em a good taste of lead before they know what hit 'em, and they'll think a second time before they try again!"

The Indians came pounding in, straight for the slight rise the cattle had used to gain the top of the butte. They were only five hundred yards away now, and the whites could see the faces and the streaming eyes of the braves as the cold winds bit into them. They were hungry and wanted food. The buffalo had been scarce that year, and the Indians were starving to death in their villages. The whites had food, and they were going to take it.

The Indians were three hundred yards away now. Sarah and Duke were side by side, and Sarah leveled the carbine. "I sure hope that heathen devil is in this bunch," she said quietly.

"One Comanche is just as good as another, Miss Sarah," Duke replied. "Ready?"

"As I'll ever be," she said.

Red Shirt had settled himself close to Sarah and Duke now and had a carbine resting on the edge of the rim. He watched the Indians swerve a little to come in line with the slope to the top. They were not going to stop, but would try to force themselves through on a hard run.

"Ready!" Red Shirt bellowed.

Up and down the rim the men set themselves, forgetting the cold now, not feeling the stiffness in their fingers, not really feeling anything as they watched the Indians enter the depression at the foot of the slope.

"Aim!" Red Shirt bellowed.

The men tightened up and set their sights on a head or chest or a side shot into the back and chest and waited. The Indians were having a difficult time getting up the first third of the slope; their ponies kept slipping and sliding on the hard earth.

"*Fire!*"

The first shots echoed through the hard, bright air as one. Five braves fell off their horses and rolled back toward the bottom of the slope. But five more took their places as the empty ponies skittered out of the way and ran off to the side. The Indians began to fire back now. Those in the rear and at the bottom of the slope took their time and aimed their carbines slowly, while others on the side began to throw shafts into the air.

Duke saw a cowboy drop silently, an arrow in his head. Another jerked up with blood pouring out of his neck where a slug had torn out his windpipe. He tried to yell, and died making the most horrible sound Sarah had ever heard.

The Indians fell back. Duke counted nine bodies that had rolled back to the bottom of the slope. Sarah and Duke continued to fire, with Red Shirt beside them bellowing at the top of his voice, urging his men on. "Shoot straight, you bastards! Shoot straight—and we'll clean 'em out!"

The Indians fell back, riding hard out of range, leaving seven dead at the bottom of the slope and taking two wounded with them.

They rode out a thousand yards and came to a stop, making a line across the plain. Even the empty ponies came to a rest, in line with the others. Several of those in the center of the line began to talk and make gestures with their arms.

Sarah dropped her carbine.

Red Shirt turned to Duke. "Want to thank you for warning us, mister. Name's Ryan."

"What you think they're going to do now?" Duke asked, nodding toward the Indians and reaching out to take the offered hand of the red-shirted Ryan. "Name's Duke, and that's Miss Sarah."

"How do, ma'am," Ryan said. He turned back toward the Indians. "They'll hit us again, but they've decided that since they lost their surprise party—they're going to hit us from front and back."

"That makes good sense," Duke said.

"For them, not for me," Ryan said.

"You could leave a few of us here on the rim and pull back with the others to the wagon and hold up any others that might come around the back."

"Might, hell," Ryan said. "There they go now." The Indians were splitting up evenly into two groups. One of them raced back over their own trail to the head of the butte where Sarah and Duke had climbed up to the flat top.

"Who're your best shots?" Duke asked, getting up suddenly.

"Ain't nobody in camp better'n me," Ryan said. "Why?"

"Two good shots could hold this rim and the rest could go back to the wagon and fort up there."

"You any good?" Ryan demanded. "Cause if you ain't, I got a boy here that could take the hair off a ant's ear at fifty yards."

"Then why not send him back to the wagon," Duke said. "He could do a lot of work back there with the others. I'll do all right up here, I reckon."

Ryan nodded. He turned to Sarah. "I'd feel better if

you'd just git in the wagon, ma'am, and not try and do any shooting."

Duke laughed. "Man, you don't know what you're saying. This woman's been looking all over creation for one special Indian that killed her husband and children. You ain't seen a woman like this one before."

Sarah appeared not to hear. She had been studying the faces of the Indians, searching the bodies of those at the bottom of the slope, looking for one with a large full nose and big hands.

Ryan backed up. "This lady ain't your wife?"

Duke's voice cracked down hard. "Not yet, she ain't."

"Okay, mister. I got enough trouble on my hands with Comanche without getting a man riled about disrespect," Ryan said and looked Duke in the eye. "All right, boys!" he yelled. "They're going to try and cut us up from the back. All you git back to the wagon and set yourself up for a long fight. These devils is hungry and they mean to go home with some cows."

The men began to pull back toward the wagon, running back in their high-heeled boots and ducking their heads against the wind.

Ryan indicated he would pull further over to the right of where the Indians would try the slope again. Duke turned and looked at Sarah. "Did you see One Nest, Miss Sarah?" he asked.

"Yes," she said. "I did."

CHAPTER FIFTEEN

THEY WAITED for more than two hours, pulling up at the edges of their jackets to fight the wind, pulling their hats low, blowing on their frozen fingers, kicking the frozen ground with their feet. They never took their eyes off the party of Indians that stood still and remained in line before them.

Ryan had bellowed for one of the cowhands to bring coffee up to the rim, and Sarah's hands were so cold she could hardly hold the tin cup. She did not drink all of the coffee. She kept half of it and stuck her trigger finger into the warm liquid, grimacing in pain when the needles started biting the flesh back to feeling. But it worked, and once she had the right forefinger loosened up, she stuck it in her mouth to keep it warm.

The sun began to beat down now and in the bright, clear day it warmed them up a little, but the winds never stopped and they could not move their positions, but had to remain belly-down on the frozen earth.

The first party of Indians remained stationary. "You'd think they don't have blood in their bodies the way they sit those ponies and take this wind with nothing more than buckskin and a blanket wrapped around them."

Without any warning, several of the Indians rode in toward the slope hard and fast, and began firing. They did not try to gain the hill; they didn't even come close enough for range of their own weapons.

"Crazy bastards!" Ryan said.

"Which one is One Nest, Miss Sarah?" Duke asked.

"That big one close to the middle, sitting the paint with the red blanket wrapped around him and the feathers flying."

"Are you sure?" Duke asked, squinting at the Indian. "I can hardly make out their faces."

"I'm sure."

Duke pulled the Sharps up and examined it. "You want to try a shot at him with this? It's got a little more range than yours."

"No, I'm going to kill him with my own gun," she said.

"Are you sure it's him?" Duke asked again. "One Indian looks a lot like any other Indian, Miss Sarah."

"I said it was him," Sarah replied and continued to stare at the line of Indians sitting absolutely still in the windswept clear blue day.

Duke settled down beside her and waited. If it was One Nest, he thought, today might be the end of the search. He turned and looked at Sarah. Then she'd be his. "Miss Sarah, I hope you git him."

"I'll get him."

There was a sudden burst of gunfire well in back of them and without turning they knew the second party of Indians was attacking the wagons and the cattle camp. Almost at once the first party broke from their solitary line before the slope and drove straight ahead. Aiming low and carefully, Sarah, Duke and Ryan began to ready themselves for the onrushing braves.

Behind them the firing began to speed up, but it was still only coming from the Indians. The cowboys were holding their fire until they could be sure of bringing something down with their shells.

The first party moved rapidly to the base of the slope and began to drive in for the ride upward. Sarah waited until she was sure. Yes, it was One Nest. She could never forget that face. Her eyes darted quickly to the Indian's hands. Yes! And the fan of black hair, shoulder-length now tucked up in a feathered headdress. She watched the face bounce in toward her. She leveled the carbine. Her vision danced. She saw the face of her son and the scalped head, and the body of Little Sue. She wiped the water out of her eyes. He was getting closer all the time. She flexed her hand and brought her finger down on the trigger. One Nest rode hard, leading the others, yelling now, his mouth open. Duke watched the Indian come forward, leading, screaming, and driving for the slope. He was torn between aiming for the head of the nearest Indian and wanting to look at Sarah.

Ryan began to fire. A brave dropped out of the saddle. The Comanches began to fire now, their bullets whistling in the air. Someone screamed near the wagon, and then there followed a furious volley of shots.

One Nest drew closer to the slope. They were at full

gallop and the shooting behind them was at its height. Ryan began to pour lead in a steady fire and a second brave slipped from the saddle.

Gibson Duke turned suddenly and looked at Sarah. She had the gun up and aimed. What was he thinking! If the Indian was killed it would be over with and they could stop the crazy search.

He clenched his teeth. He pulled down on the head of One Nest, who was within a hundred and fifty yards now. He sighted carefully. There was a sudden noise beside him and he saw One Nest slip from the saddle. He turned. Sarah had her head up over the rim and was looking down at the fallen figure of One Nest, spread-eagled on the hard ground.

"You got him, Miss Sarah!" Duke yelled. "He's down!"

Sarah did not look up or reply. She quickly aimed her carbine and fired again. Duke, his thoughts running wild, turned back to the rim and began to fire. Again and again, he fired into the line of Indians as they advanced toward the slope. Ryan's fire was steady.

Behind them at the wagon the firing had settled down into a steady pattern. The gun in Duke's hand jumped and bucked as he pulled himself up above the rim for better sighting and began wing-shooting at the passing Indians. They were milling now, wavering before the steady, sure fire of the three on the rim—and a quick glance back at the wagon area told Duke that the Comanche party was making no progress there. More than a dozen Indians had rolled to the bottom of the slope.

Ryan gagged. Duke whirled around. The red-shirted man had dropped his gun and was holding his chest. He looked at Sarah and Duke, his eyes wide with surprise. With one hand he pulled himself up straight, made the sign of the cross over his bleeding chest, and fell to one side.

Sara and Duke turned back to the rim. The Indians were bunching for a last drive to gain the slope. They fired into the line, horses and men alike, just so their slugs would find a mark.

The line wavered again and the Indians turned and dropped back to the bottom of the slope. The spread of flats before them was dotted with empty Indian ponies standing patiently, waiting for their masters to come for them. The Indians fell back slowly, retreating to the very bottom of the slope, where they began to mill around, turning their fire in a concentrated effort at the top of the rim. Sarah and Duke ducked their heads behind cover and waited for the furious firing to stop, reloading quickly and then moving back up to the rim.

The Indians were moving away. Several of them had taken the wounded on their ponies and were moving back out of range and gathering in the strays. Sarah and Duke turned their attention to the wagon. The second party had been stood off. In the distance they could see the Indians getting away from the wagon area fast.

Duke got up and ran back toward the wagon. "Stay here!" he called to Sarah.

Sarah remained still. She watched the Indians in the flats below circle and gather up the loose horses and then turn and start back down alongside the rim of the butte, moving away at a fast pace.

Sarah stood up. She looked down at the sprawling bodies of the Indians and stepped over the edge. Her eyes bright and hard, she jumped down into the slide of the slope and ran, sliding to the bottom. She moved cautiously among the dead Indians, but hurrying from one to the other. She carried her Colt in her right hand and a buffalo skinning knife in her left. One by one she turned the Indians over and looked carefully at their faces.

Duke stood on the rim with the remaining cowhands and watched her. She began to move frantically from one to the other. She began to kick the dead bodies. She began to spit on them, and then while Duke and the others watched, she slumped down and began to cry.

Several of the men started down the slope, but Duke waved them back. "She's got a reason, boys, and it wouldn't do to try and talk to her now."

Duke stood alone and watched Sarah at the bottom of the slope. They had taken One Nest with them. They had taken their chief—and there was no way of knowing if he was dead or alive.

"Cooks made some coffee, mister," a cowhand said

passing him with a horse on his way for the body of Ryan. "Damned if you don't look froze out."

Duke mumbled something. He turned slowly and walked back toward the wagon. It wasn't over. Twice now they had met One Nest and twice he had slipped through their fingers.

No, it wasn't over yet.

CHAPTER SIXTEEN

THEY HUNG AROUND the camp the rest of that day, helping to hack out graves for the five dead cowhands and Ryan. They didn't bother with the Indians. By noon the vultures began to circle and fight and wail at the bottom of the rim. One of the cowhands walked over to see what was going on and came back, his face white and drawn. He didn't speak to anyone the rest of the day.

Sarah would not speak to anyone. The men left her alone. They had too much trouble of their own to be concerned with the revenge of a woman, though one by one they came to her and thanked her for risking her life to warn them.

That night Sarah slept in the wagon, and was warm for the first time in weeks. But she was not aware of the comfort. Her eyes were hard and bright. She stared at the top of the wagon for hours, reliving the vision of One Nest riding up the hill, reliving the moment, the exact instant that she fired and trying to pinpoint the exact spot where she had hit him.

She could not say. She tried to tell herself over and over that she had hit him dead-center and that the braves had taken him only because he was their chief, but she could not make herself believe that it was true.

Was he dead or alive?

She rolled over. It did not matter. She would go on—if it took the rest of her life.

She was awake when Duke came to the end of the wagon and spoke to her. "Near day, Miss Sarah."

"Saddle the roan for me, Mr. Duke. We can't let them get too much of a head start on us, with the ground hard to leave a track in. We've got to get after them." Her voice was hard and the way Duke remembered it the first time he met her at the boardinghouse in Lister.

He knew now as he had learned in the months they had been together, there was no use in trying to talk her out of it. "Yes, ma'am, Miss Sarah. You better git up now and have a good hot meal before we strike out."

They rode out of the camp with only a nod and wave to the hands that were readying the gear for a move back into Little Ben. Duke had overheard the foreman discussing how they should tell Ryan's wife. He was glad that he didn't have to go with them.

They took coffee, sugar, and beef strips, replaced their ammunition, and dropped off at the end of the butte where they had first climbed to the top. They scouted for half an hour and found the trail and began following the Indians at a fast trot. Sarah's eyes were hard and bright and she did not talk to Duke the rest of the day. The wind had died a little, but they did not dare make a fire. They pulled at beef jerky and washed it down with ice-cold water and settled for the night against their horses. The wind picked up again about midnight and before dawn it began to snow.

"Git up!" Sarah slapped Duke's face. "The snows are coming and we'll lose their trail!"

Duke stood up and looked around him. The flats to the south had been transformed into a sheet of white. The wind picked up heavily and began to blow the snow. In half an hour there were two and a half inches of snow across the plains.

They couldn't go on; it was impossible to track anything now. But Sarah would not stop. She saddled the roan and slung into the saddle. She started out. Duke grabbed the reins and pulled the pony to a stop. "You can't go, Miss Sarah," he said firmly.

"Let go the horse, Mr. Duke," she said.

"You'll have to shoot me, ma'am," he said, looking her in the eye. He pointed to the northwest. "There's big snow coming. If we don't hightail it back to Little Ben right now and quick, the buzzards will be picking our bones clean the first hot spell."

Sarah drew the Colt and cocked it. "Let go the leather, Mr. Duke. It's going to be a hell of a lot tougher on One Nest and his Indians than on me."

"I said you'd have to shoot me, ma'am." Duke said casually, and then quickly, he jerked the pony's head and grabbed for the gun. Sarah fired, the bullet narrowly missing Duke's head.

He had the gun. She reached for the carbine in the boot. He reached up and pulled her out of the saddle, wrenching the rifle out of her hands. She struggled against him, quietly, fiercely with surprising strength. "Let me go," she said between clenched teeth. "You're going to have to let me go some time, and when you do, I'm leaving."

"Miss Sarah—" Duke said harshly. "Now you listen to me!"

"I won't!"

He slapped her hard across the face. She took it like a man and glared at him. "Don't—don't do that again, Mr. Duke."

"I will, damn it, if I have to do it all day long until you get some sense in your head."

She broke away from him suddenly, pulling back and turning to point into the thickening snowstorm. Her voice was high-pitched, but she was not hysterical. "He's out there! You hear that! He's out there—and if he ain't dead, he's wounded so bad he won't live through it. I want his hair, Mr. Duke! I want that Indian's hair, and I'm going to have it!"

Duke turned his back on her and walked back to his horse.

He climbed into the saddle and walked the pony back to the roan. 'Git right on your horse," he said firmly.

She stared at him.

"Miss Sarah, I'll go along with you on just about anything you say. I think I've proved that already. But there comes a time when common sense has to be used."

She did not move.

"Miss Sarah, either you git on your horse or I'll tie you on. We're going to Little Ben and wait out this storm. When the weather breaks, we'll go back after him. But if we don't get into cover soon, we'll be done for. Now, I'm asking you for the last time, git on your goddam pony."

Sarah wavered. She took a deep breath. Her chin dropped and she climbed back into the saddle. Duke rode up beside her and slipped the carbine back into the boot and handed her the Colt. He nudged the black and rode ahead of her to break the trail.

The snow swirled around them. Sarah could see hardly ten feet in front of her and could barely make out the outlines of Duke's back. She nudged the roan and followed, getting closer, bringing Duke's back into sharper view.

They rode all day, with the snow drifting higher and higher as they moved. It grew dark early, and soon they rode with a rope strung between them. They did not dare stop. Even if they killed the horses, they could not stop. Sarah was completely lost. She held her face buried deeply in the fleece of her jacket with her hat pulled down tightly.

She did not think. She rode with her eyes closed. Over and over she recounted the vision of One Nest riding up the slope and the moment she pulled the trigger—but she could not say where she had hit him, only that he fell.

She felt a tug of the rope and pulled the roan to the left.

It seemed to Sarah they rode endlessly, slipping and sliding, and once they walked right into a drift that was higher than the heads of their horses, but they kept moving. The snow was thickening and it was impossible to see anything at all.

Some time later, Sarah did not know how much later, she saw a light. Was it a light? She wasn't sure. She opened her mouth to call out to Duke, but no sound came. She tried again.

"Take it easy, Miss Sarah. You're going to be all right."

Sarah opened her eyes then. She saw faces staring at her. She tried to find Duke. There he was, standing over her.

"You been sleeping—" Duke stopped. "Anyway, you're all right now. Mrs. Boyd will take good care of you, and I'm here."

"I got some clear broth here for you, Miss Sarah—" a soothing voice said. "Now just raise your head a little."

"Have I been here very long?" Sarah asked, looking around the small, roughhewn, neat cabin.

"Pete pulled you two out of the storm three days ago. We didn't think you was going to make it, but praise the Lord, you're going to be all right."

CHAPTER SEVENTEEN

MR. AND MRS. BOYD had heard about the Indian fight from Ryan's hands as they passed on their way back to Little Ben. And when the blizzard hit, Pete Boyd had gone out in search of them in the hopes that they had turned back.

The blizzard blew for ten days, and for ten days Duke and Mrs. Boyd watched Sarah every minute, taking shifts, while Mr. Boyd took care of the chores. Sarah would slip into a deep sleep and remain that way for forty-eight hours at a time, then come out of it ravishingly hungry, eat everything Mrs. Boyd would give her, and then go back to sleep.

"She's worn out," Mrs. Boyd told Duke. "I never seen a more wore-out creature in my life. And I don't wonder, after your telling me you rode all the way down from Cheyenne since December!"

It took Sarah four weeks before she could sit up without help and it was toward the first of March, with the snows gone and the beginnings of the thaw coming on, that she was allowed out of bed. They had gotten a doctor in from Little Ben and he swore it was nothing but sheer guts and gall, staring death straight in the eye and spitting to boot that kept Sarah alive. Double pneumonia with complications of poor physical condition, the doctor had said flatly, on taking his first look at her.

During the first hot days of late March, Mrs. Boyd and Duke would wrap her up in warm wool blankets and carry Sarah out into the protected yard away from the wind, and let her sleep in the sun. She grew stronger with each day and Duke spent all his time away from her helping Pete Boyd with his hundred-head herd, hunting for fresh game and wild spring roots, onions, and once in a while a late flying duck as it winged its way back to the Canadian line.

The roan and the black fattened up on the steady oats and hay diet and little activity, and Duke brushed the animals until their coats were sleek and bright. The day Sarah saw the roan she cried, and pressed Duke's hand tightly.

They made friends in Little Ben. Friends and neighbors of the Boyds and the families of those that had survived the Comanche raid, and even the relations of those that had died, all came to pay their respects for the efforts Sarah and Duke had made in warning them of the Indian raid.

Duke knew Sarah was getting stronger when she began to question everyone that came out to the Boyds' about One Nest. Patiently and carefully she asked if any Comanches had been in to trade with the townsfolk and if any riders had gone through that reported anything unusual about the Comanches and their movements. She got out a piece of paper and made a crude map of Texas, particularly the Pecos River area, and began to make little X's on the places where Comanche villages had been reported, tried to get the names of the chiefs and the number in the village. But none of it, that Duke could see, helped her. No one knew anything about One Nest, and the only Comanches any of the Little Ben citizens knew about was old Kaygeesee, and he had made peace with the settlers long ago.

The red-and-gray plains gave over to the sage finally, and one morning when Sarah got up and walked to the window there was a blanket of purple as far as the eye could see.

She started to cry. She turned back to the bed and cried the rest of the afternoon. No one went near her. Duke had long ago told the Boyds about Sarah's search, and they recognized that Sarah's crying was part of her tragedy.

She came out for supper, her eyes swollen and face streaked even though she had rinsed it off with cold water. "It was a year ago," she explained, "exactly a year that I lost my family."

After they had eaten, she helped Mrs. Boyd with the dishes. The elderly woman had become more than fond of Sarah and Duke, not having any children of her own. She waited until Duke and Pete had gone out to bed down the stock and check the horses before speaking.

"Sarah, I've come to feel like you were my own daughter."

Sarah nodded. She too had grown fond of the woman who had saved her life and had been so patient with her. "I know."

"It's plain that you ain't no ordinary woman and that that Duke of yours ain't just any hand, either. You two done a lot. Only half of what you said you did this past year would fill the pages of a book."

Sarah shook her head. "I'm sorry, and please don't say it—because I would hate to say no." She hung up the dishcloth and walked to the window and looked out. She took a deep breath of the warm spring air. "You're a kind, patient woman, Mrs. Boyd—but I guess it's time for me to be leaving."

"Why? Would you just tell me why?"

"I'm going to have that Injun's hair," Sarah said in a voice so hard that the kindly Mrs. Boyd was shocked. "I'm going to cut that Injun in two with these hands." She held out her arms, browned from the spring sun.

"And what then?"

"If you still want me," she said, going to the elderly woman and kissing her gently on the cheek, "I'll be back."

Somehow the word got around Little Ben that Sarah and Duke were leaving in the morning and more than half the townspeople came to see them off.

"Where do we begin, Miss Sarah?" Duke asked.

They rode south and toward the west. "Since old Kaygeesee is peaceable these days, we might be able to trade with him a little bit and find out about the other one."

"He's on the Pecos, about a week's ride south of here," Duke said.

"That's where we'll go then, Mr. Duke."

The sleek, winter-fattened roan and black stepped lightly and with spirit in the bright spring air and the warm sun beat down on the riders and the land and seemed to be giving its blessing to the earth for shucking off the winter and surviving once more.

CHAPTER EIGHTEEN

They stood on the top of a sandy hillock and stared down into the quiet village of Kaygeesee and studied the movements of the place before showing themselves and moving down the grassy slope.

The land seemed to burst forth into life during the ride down the Pecos. Everywhere they looked was soft, shiny green and the warmth of color that is so striking in the arid lands of the big dry country of southwest Texas.

They were spotted immediately as they worked their way into the Indian village. The squaws stopped their work and watched with black, expressionless eyes. The children ran into the tipis and stared at the whites as they moved down the village street and came to a stop before a group of braves that barred their way from any further penetration ino their village.

Duke made the peace sign and spoke in Comanche. "We come to trade." He turned and slapped a duffel bag strapped on the back of the black.

The braves remained motionless. Duke turned to Sarah. "They're waiting for the old boy to come out and see if it's all right."

"How do we find out about the other one?" Sarah asked.

"Leave that to me," Duke replied quietly.

From inside a tent an old Indian dressed in snow-white buckskin with intricate, beautiful beadwork on his headband and a full bonnet of feathers, walked out and stood before the braves. "You come trade with Comanche?"

"These eyes have not seen the great Comanche chief Kaygeesee in many summers," Duke said.

The old chief nodded and Duke motioned for Sarah to get down. The old man turned and walked with stately grace through the braves and stopped before his tipi. He turned and stared at Sarah and Duke, then sank into a cross-legged sitting position. Several of the older braves joined him in a circle. Duke and Sarah sat down opposite the chief, flanked on either side by very old men.

"Kaygeesee's eyes are old, but they are still sharp as the eagle's. They do not remember seeing the white."

He said something inaudible to someone standing in back of him and the man disappeared.

"Many summers and many moons, Kaygeesee traded furs and fine skins with me."

The old chief examined him closely. "Many summers ago," he said with cold eyes on Duke, "Kaygeesee did not trade with the white!"

Duke passed it off as balm for the others sitting around the circle. The old man, Duke reasoned, had probably had a hard time getting his braves to agree to a peace agreement.

"It is told in many lodges," Duke said, "of the courageous fights Kaygeesee and his Comanche braves made with the white. There are many coups for the chief of the Comanche to talk of around the fires."

The others agreed, and the old man nodded that it was so.

Duke glanced at the others. They agreed easily, even though one Indian did not hastily call another one on his right of a coup, or the retelling of it. If there was one thing Duke admired in the Indian character it was the reluctance to brag when he recited his coups before the elders of the village. The elders were probably eager to support the old chief. If another chief took over they might be pushed out of the honored position around the fire in talks and decisions for the village.

The pipe was brought to them and one by one they smoked and passed it along. Sarah's face was immobile throughout the proceedings. Since they were not a large trading outfit, Duke asked the old chief to forego any greetings of offering of food, claiming they were not worthy of such an honor. But the old chief was not going to let an opportunity to have a party pass by so easily.

For the next three hours Sarah and Duke sat around the circle and ate and drank and watched the dances of the braves, until the sun was nearly down. The old man indicated that he was tired and did not want to trade until the next day.

Sarah and Duke were shown to a tipi and left alone.

"You think he's here?" Sarah demanded the moment they were alone together.

"No, I don't," Duke said. "And I'll tell you why. This old heathen is too old to fight and afraid of losing his place as chief, so he's bamboozled his braves into making peace—a sort of peace, anyway—with the local settlers around here. The army could probably wipe 'em out if they tried anything, and the old man probably wants to live and enjoy that fat young squaw I saw go into his tipi with him."

Duke got up and stretched and looked out the flap. No one was there. He turned back to Sarah. "It's my guess that One Nest broke away from Kaygeesee a while back and took along some of the tough young bucks that didn't like the way the old chief was running things. I looked around at their coup sticks and didn't see one new-looking scalp, that means they ain't been out on a party in some time. And One Nest was the one that made the raid against Ryan's cattle. One more thing makes me sure I'm right. That was a pretty desperate move One Nest made against Ryan and the cattle. A hell of a lot of things could have happened. The army could have clamped down on them, and they *did* lose a lot of braves and horses. But he tried it anyway, so that means his people were hungry and probably bellyaching about it and talking about how good it was back with the old chief. One Nest had to do something; and he did, he raided Ryan's cattle."

Sarah listened, and it made sense. But where was One Nest now?

"I'll find out about things tomorrow," Duke said confidently. "We'll give 'em good trades and let them think they're getting the better of us—and they'll be easier to talk to."

Sarah agreed. They settled down on the furs to try and sleep but Sarah could not close her eyes. She could not overcome the tight feeling in her stomach.

Duke traded with the Indians for more than four hours the next morning, making sure that the old chief got the best of what he had to offer and watching the old man carefully to see if his mood would change and he could engage him in conversation.

Duke had brought along a brand-new Colt with a gleaming pearl-handled butt and consistently refused high and profitable offers in furs for the gun. He saw the chief examine it with his eyes, averting them when Duke looked up, feigning indifference and aloofness with the haggle and trade.

Sarah remained in the background, stacking the furs and listening to Duke argue and haggle with the braves and watching the old man stare at the Colt. When the trading was over, the braves wandered away and left Duke to wrap up the untraded goods and store them away. The old chief's eyes hung on the pearl-handled Colt as Duke picked it up and handled it, and twirled it around his finger. He glanced up at Kaygeesee and held the gun out. "Good weapon," he said.

The old chief grunted and looked away.

Duke walked over and offered it to Kaygeesee. "See how it feels in the hand."

The old man took the gun gingerly and could not contain his enthusiasm as he examined the pistol and studied every line and mark. His eyes shone brightly.

Duke spoke softly and with feeling. "It is a gift for Kaygeesee."

The old chief looked up, stunned. "Kaygeesee could not take such a gift without equal gift in return."

Duke shook his head. "Kaygeesee does not have the eye of the eagle if he does not see the goodness in this white's heart."

The old chief wanted the gun, but he was wise enough to know that white men did not offer such a gift unless there was a motive behind it. He handed the gun back to Duke. "What does the white man want?" His voice was hard and abrupt. He settled his gaze on the middle distance and did not look at Duke again.

Duke offered the gun again. "The white does not offer false gifts."

"What does the white want?" the old chief demanded again. He did not take the gun.

Duke knew that the third time he would have to either ask the old chief the truth about One Nest's whereabouts or make up a damned good lie. "The white is looking for the outlaw Comanche One Nest," he said, and watched the old man's face.

They stared at each other a long time. "The white speaks the truth." Kaygeesee said finally, and reached over and took the gun. "The one who calls himself chief and does not listen to Kaygeesee is in the south—there." He pointed toward the Rio Grande. "He hides from the wrath of Kaygeesee."

Duke turned away and looked at Sarah. "Ready?" he asked.

Sarah nodded and they packed their furs onto the horses and climbed into the saddles. As they rode out of the village Duke glanced back to look at the old chief. Twenty-five years before he would have killed Duke and Sarah on the spot should they interfere with his hunting down and disciplining One Nest. But now the old man played with the pearl-handled gun and did not look at the white man and the woman as they rode south out of the village and a little east to pick up the Rio Grande.

CHAPTER NINETEEN

THEY PICKED UP the Rio in five days and then began following the big river, pressing hard with long rides that lasted well into the night. They made cold camps and did not take noon breaks and they avoided contact with any of the riders they frequently saw working cattle. They skirted the big ranges that bordered on the river and worked out from the spring round-ups that were taking place all over the southwest corner of Texas. Some days they rode for miles past drifting, newborn calves that stayed close to their mothers as they swung by, moving hard and fast. Not once in the whole trek down from the Pecos did they see an Indian.

The further south they moved, the hotter it became, and the light spring became the blazing heat of a hot summer. They had to halt regularly now to give the horses a breather. And one day during the heat of the afternoon Duke cut the furs from the animal's backs and left them where they lay in the dust of the south Texas flats.

They had moved down the river for nearly three weeks when they were stopped dead by a war party of Apaches that was returning with a herd of horses, and more travois dragging the dust than Duke had ever seen. There were more than a hundred mounted braves and at least that many more horses in the herd they drove, and half of them dragged booty on the tent pole travois. The dust could be seen for miles and Duke knew the Apaches would have scouts and riders out on both sides and ahead of the main party. Sarah and Duke remained where they were, not moving out of the dense thicket of brush and cactus. All one day and that night they waited for the dust to settle and the last of the Apache scouts to bring up the rear. Early the next morning the flats were clear of dust and they rode out again, beating harder trails south this time to make up for the lost time.

COMANCHE VENGEANCE 111

On the first of June they came to the Indian village. "I don't know which tipi he's in, if he's still alive," Duke said, staring down at the forty-odd scattering of tents. They were protected in front by a soft, sandy ridge and down on the other side by the thickest growth of thorny brush Sarah and Duke had ever seen. They had carefully hacked out just enough room to squeeze the horses and themselves into when a rider came out of the village and passed within fifty feet of them on his way to make meat or after an escaped horse.

Sarah had been studying the village for four days now. She seemed to see the movement in the village even when she closed her eyes at night. Four of the larger tipi were to one side. No one ever went in and they had seen no one come out. Duke guessed they might be medicine lodges or store lodges, and had suggested a plan where they might sneak into one of the larger tipi at night and at least pick up some of the talk. But Sarah would not allow him to go alone and Duke refused to let her come with him.

Hour by hour they lay in the hot sun and watched, retreating to the brush thicket when meat parties came out of the village and returned.

On the morning of the fifth day, their water began to run out.

"We have to do something, Miss Sarah," Duke said quietly. "We can't stay here much longer."

Sarah bit her lip. "You think we might be able to trade with them and find out for sure if he's there?"

"We wouldn't get within sight of the first tipi," Duke said. "Remember, we sent a few of their menfolk to the happy hunting grounds when they had us before."

Sarah nodded. She was at the end of her patience. She could readily see that it would be simple to get out, but it had taken careful watching and planning to get into the cover of the brush thicket without being seen. They might not be able to get back in.

"You got any suggestions, Mr. Duke?" she asked softly.

"I still say that getting into one of them big tipis will give us a chance at information."

"But only if we both go."

"No," Duke said flatly.

Sarah sighed. "Then we better pull out of here. The horses are going to need water tomorrow and we haven't got any to give them." She studied the ground between the sand ridge and the nearest of the big tipis. "I'll take the first watch, now, and you'll take it tonight. I'm getting tired quick these days. I guess I'm not as strong as I thought I was."

Duke glanced at her sharply. In the entire time he had been with her, he had never heard her suggest that she be given special consideration. In fact, Duke often thought of her as a man when the chores were to be done.

He slipped off the ridge and dug in deep beneath the brush, cursing under his breath when he moved accidentally into a sharp thorn. The horses had long ago learned it was better to stand perfectly still rather than move around in the confined area of the hollowed out brush. They turned to look at Duke slipping into the clearing and turned back to their nuzzling of the short grass that grew in the protected shade.

Throughout the entire time they had been studying the movement of the village, Sarah had noticed one outstanding characteristic. When a meat-making party left at sunrise, they usually returned late in the afternoon and the entire village came out to greet them. Braves' squaws, old men and women, children and dogs all swarmed around the returning hunters. When the hunters were gone for several days, the greeting was even larger.

She had seen a large party leave the village the second day they began their watch on the Indian community. If her judgment was right, and the meat party returned that day, they would try and get back before dark.

Sarah settled down to wait, hiding her eyes in the crook of her arm to avoid the midday sun, moistening her lips with as little of the precious water as was necessary.

She glanced down at the thicket below her constantly. The lower the sun dropped, the more concerned she became about Duke's waking up. If he woke before the hunting party returned, her plan would be stopped.

She drowsed in the hot sun. She closed her eyes and

COMANCHE VENGEANCE 113

watched an old squaw build up her fire, and then turn to stare into the east. More and more of the Indians began to stare into the east, as if waiting for someone.

At last Sarah saw them returning. She breathed a silent hope that their hunt had been a huge success so that the festivities would be wild.

She saw the Indians before the villagers did because of her elevation. She strained her sun-weary eyes to see if they carried meat and felt her heart skip a beat as the figures of walking braves unfolded in the distance. They had killed so much meat they chose to walk back, bringing the slain buffalo and deer on the backs of their ponies.

The closer they got to the village, the more tense Sarah became. She knew she would have only a few minutes. She had seen the squaws go after the meat before, fighting their way to be first at the select cuts of beef and hurry to the fire and begin cooking it. But there was something else that Sarah was counting on. When the braves returned, the first thing after eating, they would grab their squaws and disappear into the tipis, emerging a while later to eat more.

The party was within sight of the village now. The children and younger boys began to run out and ride out to greet the returning hunters. The squaws too ran out and shouted to the men, and to each other. Their loud laughter and squeals drifted up to Sarah and she waited, tensed up like a rattler ready to strike.

The village was nearly deserted now. The squaws were fighting over the meat, pulling the dead, bloody beef from the ponies' backs and letting it fall to the ground, where they attacked it with knives and bare hands.

Sarah moved over the ridge, open to the eyes for miles around and to every single Indian in the village if they turned and glanced in her direction.

She raced down the side of the sand ridge and dove for the bottom and a clump of brush. It was five hundred feet to the nearest of the huge tipis and she began to work her way forward, crouched low and running fast, the carbine in her hands ready to fire.

She could hear them plainly now. They were returning to the village. She got up and ran for the side of the tipi. At that moment, Duke stuck his head above the ridge and bit his tongue to keep a hoarse yell from springing to his throat.

He grabbed his Sharps and laid the barrel over the edge, openly, brazenly. He didn't care if they saw it or not. If any one of them made a move toward Sarah it would be his last move.

His mouth was dry and he could not swallow as he saw Sarah stand up full and sprint the last hundred feet and dive for the side of the tent. He saw her slip beneath it.

Sarah stood up, listening, against a thick bundle of furs. They were moving all around the tipis now. She closed her eyes and opened them in the hope of hastening her eyes into adjusting to the darkness inside the tent. The heat was unbearable. She had seen no opening in the tipi from the ridge and now she knew why no one ever went in or came out; there was no opening. The sweat began to roll off her face and down into the neck of her shirt. Slowly her eyes grew accustomed to the faint light. All around her were piles and bails of furs the Indians had trapped over the winter.

The noise outside was moving away from the storage tent now, moving, Sarah guessed, to their individual tents. She stepped to the opposite side of the tent and made a small hole in the facing near one of the poles. She peeked out. The street was still full of activity, but most of the braves and the squaws had gone to their tipis. Down at the other end of the village she could see the young boys taking the horses and the remainder of the meat down toward the pens where the broomtails and stolen draft horses were kept.

She stepped back from the side of the tent and examined the inside more carefully. There wasn't any reason that she could think of for the Indians to come into the tipi. She was safe as long as she remained quiet.

She examined the skin of the tent carefully, and at four sides made small holes near the lacings so she could see both the sand ridge, where Duke lay hidden, and the entire street of the Indian village.

She stripped off her hat and wiped her face with her

neckerchief. The heat was bad but the smell of the furs was overwhelming. She clenched her teeth and moved from peephole to peephole, examining the face of every brave she saw.

She had no plan. She did not know how she would locate One Nest—find out where he was—or if he was still alive. But she was in his village, and she contented herself with that thought.

It was full dark before Duke moved. He slipped his Sharps over the edge of the sand ridge and moved slowly, hugging the ground and stopping every ten feet or so, listening and watching the village for movement other than those of the squaws in front of their tipis and the play of the children.

It took him nearly an hour to gain the back of the tipi. He slipped his head beneath the edge and waited. "Sarah!" he whispered.

He pulled himself in and remained still. "Sarah? Answer me. It's Duke!"

Silence.

He stood up and moved around the bundles and bails of furs. He kept his Sharps up, ready, and slipped from one bail of furs to another. He stepped on something—backed up and clamped his mouth shut on a yell.

He stooped down. His hands traced out the prone figure of Sarah. He began to curse silently to himself, his fingers jerking at the screw cap of the canteen, sloshing water on her face. She began to gag and started to cough. Duke held his hands over her face and leaned down close to her. "Be quiet!"

She relaxed, and then Duke felt her raise her arm and in the deep dark saw the low flash of metal. She had lain in wait for him with a knife.

She sat up. "You shouldn't have come down here," she said.

"You talk that way!" He swore at her, his voice mean. "You must be crazy."

"I am." She stood up.

"Have you learned anything?"

"No. I have peepholes cut into the lacings around the poles and I've been watching all day but haven't seen any sign of him."

"Sit quiet now," Duke cautioned. "I'm going to look."

He slipped away from her, moved along the edge of the tent skin, and found the hole that he judged would look directly into the village street. He pressed his eye against it. The same scene that he had watched from the sand ridge. He stepped to the other holes and saw the same thing. Squaws fixing their meals before their tipis, children playing and being yelled at by the squaws and now and then a brave leaving one tipi to enter another.

He turned back to Sarah. "We're going to have to search the village," he said. "That's the only way we'll find out anything."

"You're talking foolish." Sarah said. "We've got a perfect hiding place here. You understand Comanche and can listen tomorrow. We don't even know if he's still here or not."

"As soon as the village is quiet, I'll slip out and take a look around." Duke said.

"If you go, I go," Sarah said and Duke heard that special urgency in her voice that meant she *was* going. He saw down beside her. "There isn't any use talking about it, Mr. Duke, my being here now should—"

"Quiet!"

Someone was walking toward the tipi—several of them, Duke judged. "Get back and keep down. Don't breathe!" he cautioned.

The soft footfalls stopped at the edge of the tent. Then voices began to filter through the skins. "They're coming inside!" Duke hissed.

"Why?" Sarah asked.

"Shh!" Duke listened to the deep muttering, not daring to breathe. "I can't get it. But they're talking about the furs."

There was a rustling, and Sarah and Duke knew the lacings of one pole were being unthreaded. They retreated to the furtherest side of the tipi and dropped behind a pile of furs. Duke turned quickly and pulled a bale down on top of the others to throw up a barrier between them. He pulled out his knife, and indicated that Sarah should do the same. She slipped the blade out and held it tightly.

The edge of the tipi was thrown back and the cool night air filled the tent like a blast of arctic wind. Sarah nearly sneezed.

Duke listened to the voices. And then the tipi was filled with light. Duke moved a pelt slightly and stole a look at them. Three braves were examining the furs, as if looking for something. All of them were young. One picked up a pelt and ran his fingers through the fur. "They sit here and stink and the fur becomes hard—and yet he will not let us trade with the white."

"They will be worthless if we do not trade soon," the second replied.

"Why does he hesitate?" the third asked.

"Who knows? He waits for medicine. One cannot argue with a chief who waits for medicine." They moved back toward the opening of the tent.

"We do not need medicine to trade furs with the white."

"After—" the brave said a word Duke could not understand—"he does not dare make another move without the right medicine."

"Kaygeesee waited even longer for medicine," one of them said.

"Even Kaygeesee's medicine would not have protected him at—" and again there was the word Duke could not understand.

They were outside now, lacing up the tent again.

"He's here," Duke whispered to Sarah. The word he had not understood, after much thought, he realized must be Little Ben.

They waited until an hour before dawn and then slit the tipi skin at the back, facing the ridge. They moved out quickly, the heavy morning mists drifting around them in swirls, covering their bodies in vague blankets.

They were past the three remaining storage tents and approaching one of the nearest of the tipi used by the Indians. The cookfire before the flap was out. Duke looked around for signs of a dog and, seeing none, nodded to Sarah. She took up a position on the opposite side of the flap and nodded. They both held their knives tightly.

Duke drew back the flap and moved inside, Sarah following half a second later. A man, two women and several children lay sleeping. Duke moved to the brave, dropped to his knee and pressed the point into the man's neck. The Indian opened his eyes wide, fear springing to them. He swallowed and then glanced at Sarah.

Bending low, Duke spoke to him in a whisper. "Get up and follow me—make one sound and your children die."

The Indian nodded and as he moved to get up, Duke drew his Colt. The brave stood up and stepped quietly over the body of one of the women and out into the mists. They moved back to the storage tent quickly and pushed him inside.

He turned and faced Sarah and Duke calmly. "You will die for this, white!"

Duke pulled the knife again and with a catlike motion, barely slit the skin of the brave on his right cheek. "You will be the one to die if you do not do as we say."

The Indian felt the blood and looked at it on his fingers. "What do you want?" he asked, holding his voice under control.

"Where is your chief, One Nest?"

The Indian refused to reply, folding his arms and staring at Sarah and Duke with pressed lips and calm face.

Duke lashed out with the knife again; blood flowed down the opposite cheek. The brave did not flinch. "Which of your wives do you value the most?"

The brave did not move.

"Go get the young one," Duke said to Sarah. The Indian did not move. "No—wait—get the old one!" Duke said again and the brave's face began to twitch. "It is probably his mother." Sarah had not moved.

"Why do you seek my chief?" the Indian asked.

Duke told him of Sarah's children, the boy and the girl. The Indian did not move. Finally, when Duke had finished, the Indian spit on the ground.

"Watch him," Duke said, and backed off. "If he just so much as moves an eyeball—shoot him and don't worry about the noise."

Sarah leveled the carbine and took Duke's place. The cowboy slipped out of the tipi and though it was getting light, moved to the brave's tent. He lowered his voice and spoke in gruff, garbled Comanche. "Come out here, old woman!"

He waited. There was movement inside, finally the flap was pushed back and the old woman stuck out her head. She opened her mouth to scream, but Duke slammed her over the head with his Colt and caught her before she fell. He slung her over his back and hurried back to Sarah and the brave.

He dropped the old woman on the ground and slapped her face until she began to moan and hold her head. Duke had hit her a little too hard and it took a few minutes and some of his canteen water before she regained her senses. She looked around, saw the bleeding brave and began to scream again. Duke grabbed her and slapped his hand over her mouth. "This is your son, isn't it?"

She nodded.

Duke pulled out the Colt, cocked it and aimed it at her head. He turned to the brave. "Your mother will die if you do not tell me where your chief One Nest hides like a cur!"

The brave said nothing.

Duke turned then to Sarah, who watched him without batting an eyelash. He indicated to Sarah to tie the old woman's mouth and gag her.

Sarah stepped forward and used her neckerchief for the job.

Duke now moved back toward the brave. He pulled out the knife again, turned to the woman and pointed to her son. "Your son will die—slowly—if he does not talk, or if you don't talk for him."

Duke drew the point of the knife down the long muscle of the brave's arm. Blood flooded out. The brave did not move. His mother's eyes were wide with fear.

"You want your son to die?"

She shook her head.

"Then tell me where your dog of a chief hides!" Duke demanded. "Which is his tipi!"

The brave stepped forward quickly and slapped his mother in the face. "If you speak, you will die by my hands," he said.

Duke had expected this and stepped in quickly, bringing the Colt down on the brave's neck. The Indian dropped into the bundles of furs without a sound.

Duke turned back to the old woman. "If you do not tell me where your chief is, I will kill him before your eyes."

The old woman began to cry and tried to talk.

"If you try to warn the others, I will kill him instantly!" Duke said to her and released the gag.

The old woman looked at her son and then back at Duke. "He sleeps in the white tipi—" she said.

Duke felt she was telling the truth and nodded to Sarah. She quickly tied the old woman hand and foot and replaced the gag. Duke stripped leather from a bundle of furs and tied up the brave.

They turned back to the opening and stepped outside. It was getting clear now; the mists were burning off rapidly. They moved silently and quickly down the sides of the other tipi toward the white one they knew was on the other side of the village.

There was a noise and movement to one side. Sarah whipped around and brought up her carbine. There was a swishing noise and the Indian just visible at the edge of a tipi dropped to the ground. Duke went to the side of the tent and pulled his knife out of the Indian's neck, wiping it on the man's leggings. They moved on down the middle of the village. Gradually they began to see the bleached skins of the white tipi.

They moved toward it more slowly now, with Sarah just a step ahead of the cowboy. Fifty feet away they stopped.

Someone was coughing inside the tent. Duke indicated for Sarah to move around the tipi while he moved the other way. She nodded and stepped lightly across the front flap of the tent and stood on the other side. The sun was getting ready to come up over the eastern rims now. She glanced at Duke nervously. He nodded toward the flap and pointed to the ground. He was going to wait outside and guard the front.

Sarah took a deep breath, lifted the skin flap and stepped into the darkness.

CHAPTER TWENTY

SARAH saw One Nest sleeping in the corner. He did did not move or open his eyes. She could see clearly now in the rapidly growing light.

She stepped forward and raised her gun. The Indian opened his eyes, then, seeing her and the gun, his face jerked and his eyes widened.

Sarah fired just as One Nest moved, rolling over out of the fur and blanket roll he was sleeping on. Sarah fired again. The Indian dodged around the tipi on all fours, howling like an enraged animal. He was up on his toes, bent forward on his hands like an ape, his eyes watching her. Sarah fired again just as the Indian leaped to one side. He yelled and she knew she had hit him.

She became conscious of screaming outside the tipi —and the booming of Duke's guns.

One Nest dodged again, dragging one of his legs. She had hit him, but not mortally. Sarah fired again, and the Indian dropped before her, his right arm suddenly going limp. He grabbed at her legs with his good arm and brought her down.

Sarah kicked out with her boots and caught the Indian in the face, sending him back across the tipi. He dodged again as she pulled the Colt and fired. He was slammed back against the side of the tipi and she could see blood streaming down his arms. She had hit him twice in the shoulder and once in the leg.

She stood and raised the Colt. The Indian screamed and tried to dodge away on his good leg.

Sarah hit him five times in the chest. The Indian jerked back six inches every time a slug ripped into his body.

Duke backed into the tipi, his Colt hip-high, directing his fire carefully. An arrow sang through the leather of the tipi and disappeared out the other side. Other shafts flew through the opening of the flap.

Duke dropped down on one knee. "Did you git him, Miss Sarah?"

121

"Yes."

"You going to take his hair?"

"I got it." she said.

"We better git the hell out of here, then. Make a hole in the back of the tent and go on through. Try to get to their pony—it's right in back of the tipi." All the time Duke kept firing, aiming carefully and not seeming to mind the flying shafts that whistled through the leather of the tipi.

Sarah cut the tipi skin and looked out. Two braves were waiting for her. She brought up the carbine and fell forward, hitting one in the head and wounding the other in the leg. She fired again before the Indian could get a shaft into his bow. He fell over, dead. "All clear!" she called to Duke.

He backed out of the tipi, using the Sharps now and walked upright, sighting down the barrel of the gun, making every shot count. They worked their way back to the horses.

The broomtails were broken to gunshot, but several wild shafts had wounded two of the animals and they were screaming and hobbling around in the enclosure, sending the other horses into panic.

They were inside the pen now, both their guns empty and the Indians closing in. The rain of rifle shots and arrows never stopped.

"Gimme his hair," Duke said. Sarah handed over the bloody mop of hair she had taken from One Nest. Duke slapped it on the end of the Sharps and held it up. "Load the Colts, quick, woman!"

The arrows stopped coming at them. The shots from the Comanche braves dribbled to a stop. Sarah worked frantically, loading their handguns. "Hurry, Miss Sarah, they won't stand still looking at this Indian hair much longer."

The guns were loaded. She pressed one of them back into Duke's hand and grabbed the hair of One Nest, shoving it inside her shirt.

She yelled suddenly. An arrow had gone clear through her shoulder. Duke grabbed her by the good arm and jerked her back to the horses. "Git up there, Miss Sarah, and hang on or we're done for!" He lifted her to the back of a horse and swung up behind her. The shots were getting thicker. The Indians were coming in on them fast now. Duke slapped at the little animal's flank and the beast spurted around in a circle. He reared. Sarah and Duke fell off the pony and Sarah lay still.

The Indians were on all sides of the pen now, pouring concentrated fire at the two whites. Dust kicked up around the inert body of Sarah. Duke pulled her back deeper into the pens and slapped at the horses to get them out of the way and keep them from trampling Sarah.

He caught one of the horses and lifted Sarah to its back. He swung on again, leaning low, and grabbed the rope in his free hand, holding Sarah. He wheeled the pony, his Colt up and ready.

Sarah began to moan. "Wake up!" Duke yelled at her. "Wake up and hang on!"

Sarah tried to lift her head. Duke slapped her hard in the face. "Wake up—wake up!" he shouted.

Sarah opened her eyes. She could not keep her head from swimming. She tried to hold her head up, but found it nearly impossible.

Duke was firing rapidly now—scattering his shots to keep the pressure on the Indians and throw their aim off. He knew there was little time left—and he knew that if Sarah did not come out of her unconsciousness, they would be killed in seconds.

He fired at a young brave trying to get into the pen, and saw him drop. Then there was an explosion in his ears. Sarah had brought up her Colt and fired.

"Hang on!" he said.

He leaped off the broomtail and in one step was on the back of another. "Let's go!" he shouted, and kicked the pony hard in the flanks. The little animal leaped ahead. A glance over his shoulder as they raced for the side of the pen told him that Sarah was in back of him, the arrow in her shoulder dancing crazily as the pony leaped after him.

They ducked low as they neared the edge of the pen, firing point-blank into the crowded Indians, many of them naked, most of them without weapons.

As Sarah and Duke breasted the edge of the pens, half a dozen braves rushed at them with knives and slashed at their legs, missed, and slashed the little ponies.

The plains ponies faltered, and Duke's pony went down. Sarah came alongside of him and the cowboy swung up in back of her. They had emptied their guns and there was only one chance—to run. Duke dug his heels into the pony's flanks and the horse jerked forward, knocking several braves out of the way, and broke into the village street.

Duke glanced back and saw that the other ponies in the pen were breaking free. The Indians were trying desperately to stop the runaway herd—but the tough little horses had been strung too high. They would go until they were run out, exhausted.

Sarah and Duke beat their way straight through the village. At the edge of the sand ridge, Duke saw that no one was following them.

"We going to have to git our own pony, Miss Sarah!" Duke yelled. "This horse won't last another mile!"

They rode around the edge of the sand ridge and Duke slung himself to the ground, diving into the thorny brush, not even feeling the thorns as they literally ripped the clothes from his body.

He grabbed the black and the roan and led them back to the opening, scratching the horses nearly as bad as himself. But they were fresh, and they knew their own master.

Sarah was down on the ground again, blood flowing out of her wound. Duke stepped forward and without hesitating, broke the head off the shaft and jerked the arrow out of her shoulder.

Sarah passed out cold.

Duke could hear horses now. They had managed to get some of the herd, and were coming after them. He picked Sarah up and put her into the saddle. He poured half the canteen of water over her head and slapped her face. "Wake up, Miss Sarah—you've got to ride!"

She opened her eyes. "Ride?"

Duke leaped into the saddle of the black. He leaned over low and stung the roan viciously with the end of his rope. The animal leaped forward and the thing Duke had bet on, had prayed for, happened. Instinctively Sarah grabbed for the reins and held on.

They ran north and west, leaving the shelter of the thorn thicket just as half a dozen braves rounded the edge of the sand ridge. But the Indian ponies were no match for the roan or the black.

In an hour the Indians had given up an immediate chase and capture and dropped back to track the two riders.

Duke knew they expected him to stop and rest, and because of this he rode on. He drove the roan and the black all day—right through the heat and into the dusk of night. He did not stop until he came to an outcropping of bald rock with a little water.

He shot a deer and pulled the dead animal up to the water. Then he turned to Sarah. He heated water and boiled the remains of his shirt and wiped out the wound. Then he heated his knife until the metal was cherry-red.

Sarah woke up just before he was ready to seal the wounds and Duke told her what he had to do.

"Where's the Indian's hair?" she asked.

"Here." He handed it to her.

She took it in her hands, gripping it tightly. She wrapped the fan of black hair around her fingers and gripped it until her knuckles shone white. "All right, Duke," she said.

Duke pressed the blade to the wounds, front and back, and then turned away and threw up at the smell of Sarah's burning flesh.

Sarah didn't utter a sound; she didn't even pass out.

The Indians never did come after them. They remained in the bald rocks for nine days, eating the deer and watching the southern flats for sign. Sarah was in fever for three days, and Duke had to open the wounds every hour for them to drain, but there was no sign of the pursuing Comanche.

"It's going to be ten days tomorrow, Miss Sarah." Duke said. "You got your Indian and his hair—"

"Come here, Duke," Sarah said, sitting up, a smile on her face. "Come here and sit down beside me."

Duke sat down. "It's over, Duke. The Comanche years are over."

"Yes, Sarah," Duke said softly. "They're over."

"Do you like children, Duke?" Sarah asked. "I never inquired."

"Better'n horses," he said and looked at her.

"I feel a lot stronger, Duke. Very strong."

She circled her good arm around his neck and pulled him down and kissed him. "We'll worry about a preacher later, Duke."

Gibson Duke closed his eyes. The sun came up and warmed them and the sky was blue and the land was quiet and there were no sounds except those of Sarah and Duke dreaming about their children.

To one side, forgotten, drying, fly-ridden and maggoty, the dark brush of One Nest's scalp stirred in the light breeze, was lifted up and blown back into the dry flats of the Comanche country.

Louis L'Amour

THE NUMBER ONE SELLING WESTERN AUTHOR OF ALL TIME. Mr. L'Amour's books have been made into over 25 films including the giant bestseller HONDO. Here is your chance to order any or all direct by mail.

☐	CROSSFIRE TRAIL	13836-4	1.50
☐	HELLER WITH A GUN	13831-3	1.25
☐	HONDO	13830-5	1.50
☐	KILKENNY	13821-6	1.50
☐	LAST STAND AT PAPAGO WELLS	13880-1	1.50
☐	SHOWDOWN AT YELLOW BUTTE	13893-3	1.50
☐	THE TALL STRANGER	13861-5	1.50
☐	TO TAME A LAND	13832-1	1.50
☐	UTAH BLAINE	P3382	1.25

Buy them at your local bookstores or use this handy coupon for ordering:

FAWCETT PUBLICATIONS, P.O. Box 1014, Greenwich Conn. 06830

Please send me the books I have checked above. Orders for less than 5 books must include 60¢ for the first book and 25¢ for each additional book to cover mailing and handling. Orders of 5 or more books postage is Free. I enclose $_____ in check or money order.

Mr/Mrs/Miss _____

Address _____

City _____ State/Zip _____

Please allow 4 to 5 weeks for delivery. This offer expires 6/78.

A-1

WESTERNS

☐	AMBUSH AT JUNCTION ROCK—MacLeod	P3471	1.25
☐	THE APACHE HUNTER—Shirreffs	P3479	1.25
☐	BARREN LAND SHOWDOWN—Short	13659-0	1.25
☐	BOWMAN'S KID—Shirreffs	13599-3	1.25
☐	CHARRO!—Whittington	13703-1	1.25
☐	CIMARRON JORDAN—Braun	P3201	1.25
☐	DAKOTA BOOMTOWN—Castle	P3521	1.25
☐	DAY OF THE BUZZARD—Olsen	P3530	1.25
☐	THE EASY GUN—Parsons	13712-0	1.25
☐	GRINGO—Foreman	13555-1	1.25
☐	THE GUNSHARP—Cox	13549-7	1.25
☐	HE RODE ALONE—Frazee	13581-0	1.25
☐	THE KID FROM RINCON—Moore	13612-4	1.25
☐	KING FISHER'S ROAD—Rifkin	13711-2	1.25
☐	A MAN NAMED YUMA—Olsen	13616-7	1.25
☐	THE MANHUNTER—Shirreffs	13728-7	1.25
☐	THE MARAUDERS—Shirreffs	13723-6	1.50
☐	SMOKY VALLEY—Hamilton	13677-9	1.50
☐	TO HELL AND TEXAS—Lutz	13597-7	1.25
☐	TOP MAN WITH A GUN—Patten	13705-8	1.25
☐	WHITE APACHE—Forrest	13754-6	1.25

Buy them at your local bookstores or use this handy coupon for ordering:

FAWCETT PUBLICATIONS, P.O. Box 1014, Greenwich Conn. 06830

Please send me the books I have checked above. Orders for less than 5 books must include 60c for the first book and 25c for each additional book to cover mailing and handling. Orders of 5 or more books postage is Free. I enclose $_____ in check or money order.

Mr/Mrs/Miss:_____

Address:_____

City_____ State/Zip_____

Please allow 4 to 5 weeks for delivery. This offer expires 6/78.

A-4